# The Sweetheart Is In

# The Sweetheart Is In

< stories >

# S.L. Wisenberg

TRIQUARTERLY BOOKS
NORTHWESTERN UNIVERSITY PRESS

Evanston, Illinois

TriQuarterly Books
Northwestern University Press
Evanston, Illinois 60208-4210

Copyright © 2001 by S.L. Wisenberg.
Published 2001 by TriQuarterly Books/
Northwestern University Press.
All rights reserved.

Printed in the United States of America
10 9 8 7 6 5 4 3 2 1

ISBN 0-8101-5108-1 (cloth)
ISBN 0-8101-5124-3 (paper)

**Library of Congress
Cataloging-in-Publication Data**

Wisenberg, S.L. (Sandi L.)
The sweetheart is in : stories / S.L. Wisenberg.
p. cm.
ISBN 0-8101-5108-1 (alk. paper) —
ISBN 0-8101-5124-3 (pbk. : alk. paper)
I. Title.
PS3623.I84 S94 2001
813'.6—dc21
2001000130

*For the Big Three Illinois organizations*
*that support art and artists:*
*the Ragdale Foundation,*
*Women & Children First Bookstore,*
*the Illinois Arts Council*

# Contents

*Acknowledgments  ix*

**Part One**

Big Ruthie Imagines Sex without Pain  3
The Sweetheart Is In  8
Liberator  25
Pageant  34
Brunch  40
Love  44
Living with Moranza  57
The Crab  66
The Children Who Swim from You  70
The Window of Vulnerability  73
The Average Man  79
The Last Day of the World  82
Sheets  86
Rose in Her Backyard  88

**Part Two**

In the Beginning  93
Making Heroes, Beginning with One Sentence  98
After the Procession  112
The Frog/Prince  115
My Mother's War  119
Rabbi Seeking  126
That Old-Time Religion  133

# Acknowledgments

Some of the stories in this collection were previously published:

"After the Procession": *North American Review* (July/August 1996)

"The Average Man": *Nerve* (on-line magazine; May 1999)

"Big Ruthie Imagines Sex without Pain": *Chicago Review* (summer/fall 1995); *The 1997 Pushcart Prize XXI* (Pushcart Press, 1996); *Neurotica: Jewish Writers on Sex*, ed. Melvin Bukiet (Norton, 1999)

"Brunch": *New Yorker* (January 9, 1989)

"In the Beginning": *Another Chicago Magazine* (summer 1995)

"The Last Day of the World": *Shankpainter* (spring 1991)

"Liberator": *Chicago Review* (summer/fall 1995); *When Night Fell: An Anthology of Holocaust Short Stories*, ed. Linda Schermer Raphael and Marc Lee Raphael (Rutgers University Press, 1999)

"Living with Moranza": *Other Voices* (spring 1988)

"Love": *Chicago Reader* (December 29, 2000)

"Making Heroes, Beginning with One Sentence": *Storyquarterly* (winter 1998)

"My Mother's War": *Another Chicago Magazine* (winter 1986); *The Country of Herself: Short Fiction by Chicago Women*, ed. Karen Lee Osborne (Third Side Press, 1993); *When Night Fell: An Anthology of Holocaust Short Stories*, ed. Linda Schermer Raphael and Marc Lee Raphael (Rutgers University Press, 1999)

"Pageant": *My Mother's Daughter: Stories by Women*, ed. Irene Zahava (Crossing Press, 1991)

"Rabbi Seeking": *Moment* (March 1988)

"Rose in Her Backyard": *Rhino* (2000)

"Sheets": *Cortland Review* (on-line; August 1999)

"The Sweetheart Is In": *Tikkun* (January/February 1989); *Common Bonds: Stories by and about Modern Texas Women*, ed. Suzanne Comer (Southern Methodist University Press, 1990); *Cape Discovery*, ed. Catherine Gannon (Sheep Meadow Press, 1994); *Feminism 3: The Third Generation in Fiction*, ed. Irene Zahava (Westview Press, 1996)

"That Old-Time Religion": *Indiana Review* (spring 1995)

These stories have been a long time coming; "The Sweetheart Is In" began life in an entirely different form in a workshop led by Clark Blaise in 1981 at the University of Iowa. There are many others to thank:

Constant Readers: Jennifer Berman (at all hours), Sharon Solwitz, Pamela Erbe, Dan Howell, Peggy Shinner, Janice Rosenberg, Dina Elenbogen

The late Feminist Writers Guild, especially Joyce Goldenstern

The Writer Gals, past and present: Pamela Erbe, Garnett Kilberg Cohen, Tsivia Cohen, Catherine Scherer, the late Julie Showalter, Janice Rosenberg, Terri Mathes, Joyce Winer, Peggy Shinner, Sharon Solwitz, Carol Levenson, Fran Zell, Antonya Nelson

The Evanston writing group: Fran Paden, Carolyn DeSwarte Gifford, Marguerite DeHussar Allen

Students and former students, especially: Christina Villasenor and Barbara Rose

Writers, readers, teachers and friends who have encouraged my writing and my writing self: Jan Levit Silver, Sharon and Danny Brener, Barry Silesky, Freda Gail Stern, Linc Cohen, Joan Cusack Handler, Maureen Seaton, Riva Lehrer, Jack Doppelt, Kathy Kutner Friedman, Chuck Burack, Don Wiener, Jim Bloch, Anne Redlich, Rosellen Brown, Marv Hoffman, Doug Balz, Gene Miller, Madeleine Blais, Karen Lee Osborne, Robin Hemley, Paula Barvin, Florence Weinberger, Susan B. Weston, Carroll Stoner, Phil Berger, Frieda Dean, Maria Easton, Dinah Wisenberg Brin, Wendy W. Kincaid, the late Shirley Bigbee, Mildred Liles, Susan Hahn of TriQuarterly Books, and Jesse (1987–2001) and Seth Silesky, for mental stimulation

Artist retreats: The Fine Arts Work Center in Provincetown and the Millay Colony for the Arts

And: The Wisenbergs, Finks, and Rachofskys, who never asked for a writer in the family but have been gracious about it all the same.

## *Part One*

❊

# Big Ruthie Imagines Sex without Pain

Ruthie imagines sex without pain. She imagines it the way she tries to reconstruct dreams, really reconstruct. Or builds an image while she is praying. She imagines a blue castle somewhere on high, many steps, a private room, fur rug, long mattress, white stucco walls, tiny windows. She imagines leaving her body. It frightens her. If she leaves her body, leaves it cavorting on the bed/fur rug/kitchen table (all is possible when there is sex without pain), she may not get it back. Her body may just get up and walk away, without her, wash itself, apply blusher mascara lipstick, draw up her clothes around it, take her purse and go out to dinner. Big Ruthie herself will be left on the ceiling, staring down at the indentations on the mattress and rug, wishing she could reach down and take a book from a shelf. She does not now nor has she ever owned a fur rug. But when Big Ruthie achieves sex without pain, she will have a fluffy fur rug. Maybe two. White, which she'll send to the cleaners, when needed.

She imagines sex without pain: an end to feeling Ruben tear at her on his way inside, scuffing his feet so harshly at her door, unwitting, can't help himself, poor husband of hers.

She knows there is a name for it. She has looked it up in various books and knows it is her fault. All she must do is relax. It was always this way, since the honeymoon. Of course the first months she told herself it was the newness. She is so big on the outside, so wide of hip, ample of waist, how could this be—a cosmic joke?—this one smallness where large, extra large would have smoothed out the wrinkles in her marriage bed? When all her clothes are size 18 plus elastic, why does this one part of her refuse to grow along with her? At first she thought, The membranes will stretch. Childbirth will widen. Heal and stretch, heal and stretch. But no. She has never healed, never quite healed. From anything. She carries all her scars from two childhood dog bites, from a particularly awful bee sting. I am marked, she thinks.

Ruben is the only lover she has ever had. "OK, God," Big Ruthie says, well into her thirty-fifth year, "I'm not asking for sex without ambivalence or sex without tiny splinters of anger/resentment. I am not even asking, as per usual, for a new body, a trade-in allowance for my ever-larger and -larger layers of light cream mounds. I am not asking you to withdraw my namesake candy bar from the market, to wipe its red-and-white wrapper from the face of the earth. I have grown used to the teasing. It's become second nature, in fact. And I am not asking you to cause my avoirdupois, my spare tire and trunk, to melt in one great heavenly glide from my home to yours. I am only asking for a slight adjustment. One that I cannot change by diet alone. As if I have ever changed any part or shape of my body through diet. For once I am not asking you to give me something that just looks nice. Make me, O Lord, more internally accommodating." Big Ruthie, turning thirty-five, prays. Alone, in bed.

She is afraid.

She is afraid she will lose herself, her body will siphon out into Ruben's, the way the ancient Egyptians removed the brains of their dead through the nose. Ruthie wants to carve out an inner largeness, yet fears she will become ghostlike, as see-through as a negligee, an amoeba, one of those floaters you get in your eye that's the size of an inchworm. A transparent cell. Mitosis, meiosis. She will be divided and conquered. She imagines her skin as nothing more than a bag, a vacuum-cleaner bag, collapsing when you turn off the control. No sound, no motion, no commotion, all the wind sucked out of her. Still. A fat polar bear lying on the rug. Hibernating without end. No one will be able to wake Big Ruthie or move her in order to vacuum. No one.

She mentioned it once, timidly, to the ob/gyn man. He patted her on the knee. Mumbled about lubrication. Maybe the pain didn't really exist, Big Ruthie thought. Maybe it was her imagination and this was the intensity of feeling they talked about. But it is pain. It combines with that other feeling so that she wants it and doesn't want it, can't push this word away from her brain: *invaded*. My husband is invading me. He makes her feel rough and red down there. As if he's made of sandpaper. Even with the lubricant they bought. It makes her want to cry and sometimes she does, afterward, turning her head away. How could her Ellen and Cecilia fit through there and not her Ruben?

Still Big Ruthie imagines sex without pain, imagines freedom: f——ing out of doors. In picnic groves. She imagines longing for it during the day, as she vacuums, sweeps, wipes dishes, changes diapers, slices cheese for sandwiches, bathes her daughters, reads them stories. She imagines it like a tune from the radio trapped in her mind. It will overtake her, this sex without pain, this wanting, this sweet insistence. A rope will pull her to bed. Beds. Fur rugs. Rooftops. Forests, tree houses. She imagines doing it without thinking. Her family does nothing without thinking, worrying, wringing, twisting hands, with a spit and glance over the shoulder at the evil eye. At Lilith, strangler of children, Adam's first wife, who wanted to be on top. Who wanted sex without pain. Whenever she wanted.

Sometimes Ruthie begins. She might tickle Ruben. She might hope: This time, this time, because I started it, we will share one pure, smooth sweep, one glide, a note a tune a long song, as sweet as pleasant as a kiss. She thinks, if she can conquer this, get over this obstacle, she of two children, a house, and a husband—if she, Big Ruthie, can find her way to this sex without pain—then Ruben would be able to rope her, he would be able to lasso her from the next room, from across the house. She would begin to rely on him, and on sex, on sex without pain. Then any man would be able, with a nod of his head, a wink of his eye, to pull her to him. Ruthie and Anyman with a fur rug, without a fur rug. Big Ruthie will advertise herself: a woman who has sex without pain. She will become a woman in a doorway, a large woman blocking a large doorway, foot behind her, against the door, a thrust to her head, a toss, a wafting of her cigarette. Big Ruthie will start to smoke, before, after, and during.

Nothing will stop her. She will be expert. Till she can do it in her sleep. With her capable hands, with her ever-so-flexible back, front, sides, mouth. With the mailman, roofer, plumber; she could become the plumber's assistant, he, hers. She will go at it. She will not be ladylike. She will be a bad girl. She will swing on a swing in a goodtime bar. She will become a goodtime girl, wearing garters that show, no girdle at all, black lace stockings rounded by her thighs and calves, brassy perfume that trails her down the street. People will know: That is Big Ruthie's scent. She will have a trademark, a signature.

Big Ruthie, the goodtime girl.

Fleshy Ruthie, the goodtime girl.

Bigtime Ruthie. Twobit Ruthie.

Ruthie knows that other people have sex without pain. Men, for instance. Ruben. She has watched his eyes squint in concentrated delight. She herself sometimes cries out, the way he does, but she knows his is a pure kind of white kind of pleasure, while hers is dark, gray, troubled. It hurts on the outside just as he begins and moments later when he moves inside her. This was Eve's curse—not bleeding or cramps, not childbirth, but this—hurts as much as what? As the times Ruben doesn't shave and he kisses her and leaves her cheeks and chin pink and rough for days. But this is worse.

If she could have sex without pain, she would have sex without fear, and without fear of sex without pain.

Then the thought of no sex at all would make her afraid, more than she is now of sex with pain, more than she is afraid of losing her body, more than she is afraid of never losing it, never being light.

Ruben said once she was insatiable. This is because she squirmed and writhed, wanting to savor everything, all the moments that led to the act; she wanted to forestall the act of sex with pain. When she has sex without pain, she will go on forever, single-minded of purpose. One-track mind. She is afraid she will forget everything—will forget the multiplication table, the rule for *i* before *e*, to take her vitamins, when to add bleach, how to can fruit, drive, run a Hadassah meeting using *Robert's Rules of Order*, bind newspapers for the Scouts' paper drives, change diapers, speak Yiddish, follow along in the Hebrew, sing the Adon Olam, make round ground balls of things: gefilte fish, matzah balls. Ruthie will become a performer, a one-note gal, one-trick pony, performing this sex without pain, her back arcing like a circus artist on a trapeze, a girl in a bar in the French Quarter. "You cannot contain yourself," Ruben will say, turning aside. She will feel as if she is overflowing the cups of her bra. Her body will fill the streets. People will say, "That Ruthie sure wants it."

She tries to avoid it. So does Ruben. They are sleepy. Or the children keep them awake, worrying. There is less and less time for it.

When they travel and stay in hotels, the girls stay in the room with them, to save money for sightseeing. Ruben still kisses her, in the morning and when he comes home from work, after he removes his hat.

But if she and Ruben could have sex without pain, there would be no dinner for him waiting hot and ready at the table. Big Ruthie would ignore all her duties. She would become captive to it. Body twitching. Wet. Rivulets. She would no longer be in control. No longer in the driver's seat, but in back, necking, petting, dress up, flounces up, panties down or on the dash, devilmaycare, a hand on her ————. "Sorry, officer, we had just stopped to look for—." "We were on our way home, must have fallen asleep—."

Sex would become like chocolate fudge. Like lemon-meringue pie. Like pearls shimmering under a chandelier. Or van Gogh close enough to see the paint lines. Blue-gray clouds after a rainstorm. Loveliness. Would Big Ruthie ever sleep?

*Big Ruthie's life will become a dream, a dream of those blue castles with long mattresses she will lie across, will f———k in, far away, will never ever come back from, the place high on the improbable hill of sex without pain, the impossible land of sex without pain.*

*There in the castle she will find the Messiah himself. He too is insatiable. She will welcome him inside her. She will long for him, miss his rhythms, when he departs her body. Up there in his castle, she will keep him from descending to do his duty for at least another forty years. In his land of sex without pain, she and he will tarry.*

# The Sweetheart Is In

### What the Boys Were Like

They were all over Ceci Rubin's house, swarming like bees around her sister Ellen. Though her sister was not the kind of flower you might think; even though Ellen was Sweetheart of the Senesh boys' group, she was a Nice Girl. She needed to be met two-thirds of the way in order to flirt. Had to be coached. Did not bat her eyes with frequency or naturalness. Did not laugh with the requisite ease; it was always a nervous giggle, an internal clattering of the throat muscles.

But this is about Ceci. And the boys. The boys did not swarm to the playroom, lean over the pool table, twist handles controlling the little men on the Foosball game, in order to see Ceci Rubin. She was another accoutrement of the house, like the playroom itself. For them, finding an extra girl in the home of their Sweetheart was like any other pleasant surprise—like finding someone has a wonderful dog so friendly and shaggy it bridges all conversations, or a mother who listens to problems and sings bawdy songs (only an example; no mother like that existed in Houston in 1970, in that neighborhood at least), or a father who gives advice about something useful—not as personal as sex but, for instance, about car insurance or avoiding the draft. Ceci's father was in the bubble-bath business and handed out samples to all the boys each time they came over. He'd shake their hands first.

The boys fascinated Ceci. They leaned and lounged like cats and were just as mysterious to her and to Ellen, who had always had as pets beagles and sea monkeys, nothing in between. The boys would sprawl on the love seats (everything had a name; there was not simply furniture in that house but buffets, davenports, credenzas, and islands), talk one moment about the rubbers in their wallets, the next about ways to avoid the draft—both suggesting realms that were strange to

Ceci. Ricky Bogen was seventeen and a half and was already thinking of joining the Coast Guard. He'd called the office once for brochures. Dan Cook knew a guy who'd drunk ten cups of coffee in two days, swallowing five tablets of NoDoz with each, and had been so jittery and nervous and produced such contaminated piss that they got him out of the recruitment center fast, almost calling an ambulance, and speaking of piss, Sam Frederickson's older brother had bought some from a diabetic hanging out in front of the center. Rob Chazin was applying to rabbinical school, even at this early date, and Joe Amos was reading everything from Maimonides to St. Augustine (even though Peter Griswold said Augustine was irrelevant to Jews) in order to fill out conscientious objector forms. He'd already had an appointment with his rabbi. Who'd Been in Korea, so that didn't help much.

Ceci, listening as she looked for some string in the drawers of the nearby built-in buffet, didn't quite understand this Being in Korea, thought maybe it was a metaphor, like in English class, maybe for venereal disease? She tested it on her tongue and, in a few minutes, said to Sam: Korea like in the Korean War? Yeah, Babe, he'd said, and that Babe was enough to give her tingles up until the time she brushed her teeth and fell asleep.

### How the Boys Sounded

The boys were noisy in their machines, no matter what the machine was. Even if it was a bicycle. They scraped the kickstands against the cement of the driveway, scraped them up to the front door (bikes, even fancy European ones, were not allowed indoors on the highly polished and buffed terrazzo). And cars—! They zoomed in doing something with the exhaust or the muffler, Ceci wasn't sure what it was called, to make their presence known. Then the honks. Each boys' group had a certain honk pattern which the members pounded out while passing by the home of a member or a Sweetheart. The one for Senesh was Come-out-come-out-you-son-of-a-bitch, but for the sake of appearances and parents it was Come-out-come-out-wherever-you-are. The cars were crucial. In Ellen's scrapbook was a photograph of an unidentified odometer showing 1803.00 miles, which was the Senesh chapter number. Ceci was unsure how the chapters were assigned these numbers; this whole boys' club business, she was apt to say, is beyond me. Ceci had elements of an old lady to her. She stopped just short of being fussy. She was serious and studious and fancied herself deep but laughed often, mostly to herself. But since the boys had been coming around, she had begun to laugh more in public. With the boys, she didn't have to play dumb, which she'd been doing since fourth grade. The boys of Senesh really wanted to know her thoughts. They saw her as some artifact, encouraged her to be devil's advocate, praised her when she asked: If I killed my sister—or you—while you were standing right here, it would be wrong, so how could any war be justified? Someone left behind a copy of St. Augustine's just-war theory, and she read it in one night. Sam mentioned Thomas Merton, and she went to the Meyer branch library to check out his books.

They encouraged her, called her St. Cecilia, and Joe Amos sang the Simon and Garfunkel song to her: Oh Cecilia, I'm beggin' you please from down on my knees. Other times he would call her Dorothy Parker and require a pun before they could have a normal conversation.

I am truly changed, Ceci would think to herself. I am no longer shy. But Ellen still called her the Pain. When Ellen wanted her to leave the room, she would say, Ceci, go breathe.


### What This Breathing Business Was

It began when Ceci was born and she was taken right away into a special room called I See You—this is how she had heard the story, ever since she was a little girl.

She was in ICU for two days, deprived of mother's milk and mother's love, though the nurses were quite attentive and one even sang songs to her. Christmas songs, it turned out, but the family was not that particular, no worry about imprinting. Just as long as she was kept company by another warm human voice, they said. They prided themselves on their rationality. Ceci's parents kept kosher and went to shul often, especially whenever they knew the family of the bar or bat mitzvah. They were modern Jews, observed and performed the mitzvot that made sense. Though there was behind everything—so faint you could barely feel it—a strong belief in God the primitive goat-bearded deity of the Old Testament. He hovered. He took note of their Shemas they said every night before going to sleep.

As she grew older, Ceci's lungs cleared, but they never really cleared up. She would breathe fine, then it would start up—never an attack, she hated that word, but more like an advancing case of the flu. So she couldn't run very hard or jump rope, because that would bring on the wheezing. In her childhood, as she said, she stayed inside, read, painted at the easel in her room. Mixed colors again and again, watched them swirl in the blue enamel pot of water. Like cream disappearing into coffee, changing it to cream and coffee. Coffee with cream.

When Ceci was eleven, two years before Ellen was made Sweetheart, she'd had pneumonia so bad she'd had to spend four days in the hospital. She came home with a breathing machine the size of an old-fashioned radio. She filled it with distilled water and liquid bronchodilators morning and night, breathing in the mist for twenty minutes. It made what she'd just heard called white noise. Drowned everything out.

With handheld sprays and pills and the machine, though, everything was A-OK, under control. Next semester, said her doctor, she could take gym for the first time in two years. Partly she dreaded this because she'd never properly learned the games the teachers expected her to know: softball, volleyball, and badminton. She'd never quite got the hang of team lines.

In the meantime, no one could tell anything was wrong. Couldn't (usually) hear her wheezing. Under control. Like anybody else.

### What Ceci Did with the Boys

Once one of them stayed even after Ceci told him at the door that Ellen wasn't in. They played a round of pool and he won handily. He taught her wrist action in Foosball. He told her about his application for Harvard, the grueling half day of SAT testing, told her that he thought he might be a conscientious objector. Oh I know about that, she said; CO. She'd read about Quakers being COs in World War I.

Nowadays you had to get a draft board to approve it. She knew some people Up North had poured their blood over the draft-board file folders. But not in Houston.

The boy's name was Jerry Schwartz. His brother was at Stanford, living in a co-ed dormitory and being part of the Movement. Ceci imagined him there among palm trees, studying, shouting, learning about Europe.

When Jerry left that afternoon, he said, Fair Lady, I doff my hat to you (though he wasn't wearing one), and shook her hand, lingering over it so long that she thought he was about to take it to his lips. But he didn't.

### What the Parents Thought of This Sweetheart Business

They were proud but befuddled. They'd always said it was important for their girls to have friends in the Jewish community. But they were not quite used to these long, loud boys. The Rubins didn't have norms for boys. Their directives boiled down to geography. The boys couldn't smoke in the house. The backyard was OK, as long as they put out the butts in the ashtrays of their own cars. They weren't supposed to step one foot into Ellen's bedroom. Though they did troop there sometimes, in a group. It was there that Ellen kept the large brown-spotted stuffed salamander the boys of Senesh had special-ordered for her. There was another salamander, made of plywood, that stood on the windowsill in the den and faced the circle driveway. It balanced on its tail and wore a sly grin. On its stomach were the words THE SWEETHEART IS . . . Screwed into its joined front paws was a hook which held a cardboard square. On one side the square said IN; on the other, OUT.

Ellen always forgot to change it. Ceci thought of making it say IN when Ellen was out so the boys would come in and spend time with her. Hadn't she read in *Little Women* that Mozart or Shakespeare had tried for one sister and gotten the other one? There was also Jacob in the Bible, wasn't there? She remembered something about a wedding, and Jacob (or Isaac?) hadn't been allowed to lift up the heavy veil and see who was under there until after the rabbi had already pronounced the words. And then it was too late.

### How Ellen Was Crowned and Chosen

It was at the Sweetheart Dance. It was a surprise, but Ceci and her parents had been alerted and stood there in the back, sneakily, hiding in shadow. When her name was announced Ellen fainted. Ceci, hardy in all parts of her body except the lungs, envied Ellen her ability to faint at crucial moments, a coda to underscore the specialness of events. After the dance, Ellen and the boys and their dates went to the IHOP (Ceci heard later) and ordered breakfast to go, drove to Galveston, and ate soggy pancakes on the beach. Someone brought a bedspread to sit on.

At dinner the next Friday night, Ceci's grandmother said she did not like this at all. For fifteen years she'd been a guest in that house for the Sabbath meal. She could not imagine anyone finding the sunrise something to go to, like a movie or symphony. She told Ceci's mother: A waste, a waste it sounds to me. Ceci's mother worried but found it impolite to worry in front of other people. Of course the thing that no one said but everyone thought about was the impropriety of boys and girls of a certain age traveling unsupervised to another town, another county, the untamed ocean overnight. The overnight part. That's what they're doing now, Ceci's father said mildly. He was modern and trusted the mores of the age and therefore individuals because he could not conceive of them violating the norms. After all, this wasn't Chicago or New York, and these boys and girls Ellen was friendly with were honor students, not hippies or zippies or whatever. Ceci's mother didn't trust anything but convention. And not even that. But she was afraid to say so.

### What Ceci Knew

In Ellen's diary, Ceci had read the cold hard facts: Ellen's best friend Naomi had swum naked with not one but three boys. The diary was kept locked, but easily opened, inside an oversized photo album on a bookshelf. Ceci wondered if like the character in the book *1984* Ellen kept a hair or something equally minute between the pages to determine whether the diary had been tampered with. But it was Ceci's firm belief that Ellen secretly wanted her to read it—even if only for the challenge of catching Ceci giving herself away by releasing a bit of information in conversation that could have been obtained only from the diary.

Ellen was rather reserved in what she revealed about herself in the diary—as taciturn as she was in person. Once Ceci had asked her if she'd ever French-kissed, and Ellen, embarrassed, an edge of incredulity in her voice, responded: Ye-ess! She would not elucidate.

This sex business was something Ceci didn't think about concretely. She figured it was something like New York City—big and confusing and exciting. The mystery at hand was smaller and closer: periods. There were tantalizing light blue boxes under the sink in her parents' bathroom and pink ones in the bathroom she shared with Ellen. Ceci had not yet begun. She waited for it, mistaking stomach cramps for those kind. She would see Ellen's sanitary-napkin belt hanging on the towel rack, and twice in the school bathroom she had unwrapped the cotton-and-blood jelly rolls in the steel basket attached to the wall and smelled the rust-iron personal foreign blood.

At night, Ceci had a more than dimly related secret habit. She rocked quietly in bed, thumb against that ridge of flesh, until she felt a turnaround unwinding feeling. She'd been doing this for years and thought it was something that only little girls did, something like holding on to your baby blanket too long. Next time, she'd think, I'll stop.

### What Ceci Worried About

She was afraid that she wouldn't do the exciting things life owed her. Afraid a boy wouldn't love her and kiss her. Afraid she'd be too tall all her life. Afraid she wouldn't be famous. Afraid her feet would never stop growing. Afraid she'd be ugly forever. (She didn't believe her mother when she called her beautiful.) She was confident she'd get into a good college Up North. She did well on standardized tests. She hadn't told Jerry Schwartz that, he with his reports of grueling APs and SATs.

She was afraid her best friend Sheryl Lefkowitz didn't really like her as much as she liked another girl, Annie Kaplan, who went to a different junior high. She was afraid of being abandoned. She feared and anticipated returning to gym classes. She imagined that her return would mark an opening in her life—she would pick up everything she had missed and forge unbreakable bonds. Because surely it was in the locker room that these alliances were formed: the invitations to walk home after school, to go shopping for shoes and purses at Palais Royal, to go get haircuts, to look up *Everything You Always Wanted to Know about Sex* at the Meyer library, to spend the night out.

She felt both older and younger than her friends. Sheryl Lefkowitz, for example, was already ahead of Ceci in some departments. She had let a boy feel her breasts. She told Ceci about a girl giving what was called a hand job. Ceci wondered how these girls knew what to do. She would have no idea. She'd heard that once you started they wouldn't let you stop until the sperm came out of there, and some of them made you drink it.

### How Ceci Was with the Boys after a While

Ceci began to feel adopted by them. They took her bowling and one night got her drunk on André Cold Duck at Joe Felts's house (his parents were gone) and she sang songs with them, making up the words. Ellen got mad. Ceci didn't care. The boys were very careful with her. They did not, for example, have her sit on anybody's lap, the way they had girls their own age do. They made a joke: Sit on my lap and we'll see what comes up. She didn't get it, but knew it was not something her mother would want her to laugh at. Just like the jokes they made about the pool-table balls.

She helped Jerry Schwartz make up the creative services for Senesh Sabbath Morning with Herzl girls' group. They chose works, as Jerry called them, by Eugene O'Neill and Leonard Cohen and the Beatles. This excited Ceci. She had not known that Jews could pray by reciting Blackbird singing in the dead of night. He showed her a poem by W. H. Auden: Poetry makes nothing happen. He explained that people have to do things in the world. He talked about the Chicago Seven trial; she'd seen a TV screen full of hippies with long dark hair making peace signs. He explained the difference between hippies and yippies. (No such thing as zippies, he said.) He told her about his underground paper at St. Mark's, a private school in River Oaks. His family lived near Rice University. She knew that Jews couldn't live in

River Oaks unless they were very very rich, because of covenants and deeds. He brought her a copy of his paper with reports about Vietnam and protests and editorials with cusswords. The typing was low quality and so was the reproduction. He told her she could keep a copy. The mimeographing ink came off on her hands.

### How Ellen Felt about All These Developments

She was mad. Said the same thing she said when she was seven and Ceci was three: Ma-a, tell Ceci to play with her own friends.

### How Ceci Entertained Another Boy

Tom Hessler rang the bell even though the brown-spotted plywood salamander in the window said OUT, and he and Ceci made mint brownies even though her mother had told her not to do any baking because she needed the kitchen at five. Her mother was mad, but only for a few minutes. Tom took half of the batch home (that had always been the house rule—share with the guest baker), wrapped in foil.

Late that night he fed one into his girlfriend's mouth, lightly flicking the dark crumbs from the corners of her lips. The girlfriend said, Mmmm, mmm, my favorite, chocolate! And he said in a high voice, Mmm, mmm, you're my favorite! and nibbled at her lips.

Tom didn't tell this part to Ceci when he played Foosball with her a week later. All he said was that his girlfriend would only eat one brownie because of her dy-et. Ellen was standing next to him as he was saying this, and he turned to put his arm around her lazily. For some reason he was thinking of Bogart at this moment and turned to Ceci and said, Game's over, get lost, kid. The next time Ceci saw him he put his arm around her that same way. She tried to bite his hand and was embarrassed at how desperate it seemed, not at all playful.

### How Ellen the Nice Girl Got to Be Sweetheart in the First Place

Ellen was not a tart. When she was just a civilian, back in tenth grade, she'd had one good friend who was a boy; he'd moved to town from Dallas at the end of a semester, and she'd been nice to him because she was nice to everyone, especially new boys in her homeroom. He became popular and persuasive. He joined Senesh that summer. The other boys in Senesh wanted to elect one of two girls who were Class A Number One flirts, supreme gigglers, and hairtossers. Ellen was the dark horse, the spoiler. She won the election. She was pretty, so no one really minded. She was like a sleeper movie. By the time people have seen it, they feel bad that, but for a quirk, they might have missed it. And so they feel doubly grateful.

### What Ellen's Manner Was

She would say Hello, how are you? and would make a reference, as the girl-gets-boy guidebooks suggest, to something the boy had mentioned the day before. She began to read the sports pages, to talk about the Astros' chances for the pennant. The boys were nonplussed. They'd never heard of girls who knew about sports. They'd say, like indignant fathers, Now what do we have here? But they were pleased. They congratulated themselves on their choice. They began to say, Hay as in horses, we sure know how to pick 'em.

Ellen was the supreme democrat. No one boy got more attention than any other. She regulated her inflections. She became all things to everyone. A queen. Dabbing the foreheads of the dying teeming poor camped at her gates. She became more and more aloof. And therefore more disinterested. Which is not the same as uninterested. And thus more and more fair.

### What Ellen Did to Herself

She took hair from the top of her head and rolled it around two empty orange juice cans, wrapped the rest with oversized bobby pins and oversized clips, and sat under the dryer for two hours (so adept at this that she could hold telephone conversations while under the hood with other girls similarly encumbered). She shaved her armpit hair, her leg hair, plucked her eyebrows, curled her lashes, applied a silver or blue-silver or gold Yardley face mask once a week, and used all manner of creams and astringents and henna hair lighteners and straighteners at various intervals.

Ceci tried to emulate, hoping for her underarm and leg hairs to darken and lengthen so she could rid herself of them. She bought her own Clearasil tube (cherishing that pasty smell), awaiting pimples, was elated when Ellen showed her the hiding place of blackheads: the crease between lip and chin.

### What Ceci Learned from Ellen and Others

The Surfer Stomp. That you were supposed to be afraid of boys. That you didn't go to second base until the fourth or fifth date at the earliest. That you were always supposed to say no at least twice to new ventures of the flesh. That no one wore tampons.

Also: Don't call boys (her mother said), boys don't like to be chased. Study their interests. Plan your makeup color scheme to coincide with and complement your clothing scheme, which means planning ahead on the little charts provided by the teen magazines.

### What Happened When Mr. and Mrs. Rubin
### Went Away for a Marketing Convention

The boys were like an occupying army. They ate Golden Delicious apples from the drawer in the refrigerator and picked tangelos from the backyard and poured themselves mixed drinks. They tracked in mud and seemed to have no homes of their own. They were dark and alive and loud.

Sam Frederickson and Joe Amos left behind on the antique davenport a tape cassette from their legendary Sam and Joe I Won't Go Show. Ellen left with them to go to a meeting. As they were shutting the door, Joe said, Don't wait up for her. They all three laughed. Ceci made herself a tuna melt, loaded the dishwasher. Her homework was finished. She had no one to call. Her hair wasn't dirty enough to wash. She took her parents' old copy of *The Group* (She can read anything she wants, her father would say, if she doesn't understand it, it won't hurt her) and leafed through it while she breathed on her machine. She wanted to be with people. She wanted talking.

Don't wait up for her, Joe had said. Ceci took the boys' tape and rewound it to the beginning and brought it to the bathroom. She turned on the bathwater.

Sam and Joe were singing the antiwar song they'd made up: Ain't no use to wonder why, I think I'm gonna die—and it's five-six-seven open up them pearlized gates—. Then they trailed off to advertise an upcoming interview with the Ass-Tit Jewish-American Indian Princess who showed off her wares to the poor boys in boot camp in Butt Butte, Wyoming. The field of Ceci's mind was an expanse of far-reaching cities and villages real and imaginary, but she had not thought of Butt Butte. Though she had had those kinds of images when she was in her bed, rubbing with her thumb. Or in the tub.

She ran more warm water over a handful of Barnston's bubble powder and imagined the Ass-Tit Princess, greeted by the cheering invading army of Salamanders, boys touching her breasts shed of their loincloth just for them, the eye of her tit warmed in someone's eyeless hand. Someone's cheek and lips, and she was the princess and the hand and the hands.

Ellen had not mentioned to Ceci any Indian princesses or do-it-yourself thumb projects of her own. Ellen wouldn't, Ceci thought. She was the Sweetheart and she was four years older. Besides, she hadn't mentioned it in her diary. The juiciest thing Ceci had read in Ellen's diary was about Ellen's friend Naomi.

Ceci thought of Naomi, naked, water streaming over her shoulders and swishing her pubic hair. Like seaweed. Mermaids. She wondered if Ellen did that too. That overnight in Galveston with the boys and pancakes—.

(Always the baby, the one it doesn't matter if she's wearing her robe and two orange juice cans on her head, she's the baby, the one who doesn't count, the one too young to go out with. You, Ceci, go and get the door and tell them I'm almost ready, Ellen would say. Entertain them. But not too much. Make them laugh once.)

Ceci in her tub filled with bubble bath from her father's factory imagined a dance-hall hostess knocking and not noticing Ceci, and lying on top of her, still not feeling her, then a man coming in the door and soaping the lady on top of Ceci. Ceci would stay so so quiet because she finally would learn something, here was her chance. She began to hum. Quick—she thought she heard Ellen unlock the back door and Ceci reached over and stopped the tape (thinking: Thomas Merton was electrocuted in his bathtub) and jumped out to turn on the radio real loud, KPRC, news and talk.

### What Ceci Knew about the War

That it was wrong. The government was wrong but mostly only the Jews and Northerners and Catholics and students in California knew it. Jerry's underground paper was against it from the word Go, and it also editorialized about, as he called it, concerns of its constituency. It editorialized against the uniforms they had to wear in his private school. One day he organized almost everybody not to wear a tie. They won. Now every Friday they could leave the ties at home. It was a great victory. But Jerry said he felt uneasy about it. The principal had given in too quickly.

### How the News Came to Ceci's Class

There was some sort of murmuring, the sort of buzz that precedes a big announcement. The history teacher, Mrs. Thompson, was late to class. She said there would not be a quiz but to prepare for a discussion on the League of Nations. Then she left. While she was gone Joel Arner and Jimmy Buxbaum covered the entire two boards with ticktacktoe grids. Mrs. Thompson returned and announced, All right, class. There will be a pop quiz. Then she lowered her voice and looked furtive. She told them: Four students in Ohio were killed in a protest against the war. They were wild, she said. They burned down a building.

Did they have weapons? Joel asked.

I think so, she said. Yes, definitely. They attacked officers of the National Guard.

Ceci wondered if that was what Ricky Bogen was going to join. She imagined him lying down dead. But those weren't the ones who'd died. The ones who'd died were college students. Up North.

She imagined herself, a college girl, lots of dates, boys carrying her books, boys running fingers through her hair, which had somehow changed to blond and straight (you could accomplish great transformations in college), laughing, maybe a little lipstick, long lashbuilding mascara with those little hairs in the wand, blue eyeshadow, laughing and talking about philosophy. My philosophy of life, the college Ceci would be saying, is helping people. Get to know everyone. She would be walking on a campus green, by old-fashioned Old English buildings. And then the boy on her right, call him for the sake of argument Barry or Jerry, would be shot. Blood on his lumberjack shirt. Jerry Schwartz, blood on his salamander T-shirt, coming out of the paw.

The report I heard in the teachers' lounge, said Mrs. Thompson, is there were two boys and two girls.

A college girl, Ceci thought, putting her hand to her heart, and could almost feel the wet blood trickling. She wondered if she would have her period by then. Of course of course. By then it would be old hat. She thought of the X's she would make on a wall calendar. But for nothing. Blood all over the Indian princess, down her seaweed hairs, old hat by then too. She, Ceci, fallen on the grass in front of three-story stone college buildings that looked like Steak and Ales.

It wasn't my fault, she said to herself. It wasn't the students' fault, she said in a whisper. They didn't do anything wrong, she said loudly and evenly, loud as a boy.

Then she ducked her head and shakily wrote her name and "Pop Quiz #5" on the looseleaf sheet.


### What Happened at Home

The phone was ringing. Right off the hook, Ceci thought to herself. Jerry Schwartz said, Hello, did you hear? She said, This is Ceci, this is me, not Ellen. He said, I know. Did you hear? Did you hear?

Yes, she said, yes, the college students. Ellen's not here.

He said, I have the car. I can come by—

Out of some instinct, some sense of propriety, she said, I'll meet you at the JCC.

She knew it took ten minutes to walk there. It would take him at least that long to drive. Walk slowly and carry a big stick, she thought. Walk slowly and your lungs will be friends with you forever. No flare-ups.


### How They Were at the JCC and in the Car

He was on the steps waiting. Eyes kind of red. You need Murine, she thought. Once at Bruce Gottschalk's house, Bill Somebody had splashed Murine up and down his face, turned off the lights, and shined a black light on his face. The Murine tracks were purple. Everyone had said, Psy-cho-del-ic.

At the JCC Jerry said, I'll take you to my house.

Some alarm started to go off in a far reach of her mind. No boys in her bedroom. But could she be inside a boy's house with him?

Maybe the front steps.

The car radio was full of bulletins and music: Open up the pearly gates—. That's Sam and Joe's song, Ceci said, except I don't think the words are the same, exactly. How did that get on the radio? Jerry laughed, not turning to her. That's Country Joe McDonald. He sang that at Woodstock. You thought those two clowns wrote it? They couldn't write their way out of a paper bag. They couldn't even get the lyrics down right on that stupid tape they made.

She absorbed this.

### How They Were at His House

The TV was on, and the radio, on KILT, old music—"Dead Man's Curve." It was dark, the glow of the TV on a braided or brocaded couch. Kleenex in a wad. Tennis shoes in a corner. Newspapers awry. I wanted to tell you this, he said. He sat her down on the sofa. His finger brushed past her ear. She felt it, felt it more right afterward. One two three four seconds later. Still. Two-four-six-eight. Why don't we defoliate. Like a shadow touch. Look at this, she thought. He's angry about the students at Kent State but there are tears in his eyes. She was afraid he was going to sob. He took an envelope from his back pocket. He was wearing jeans. Must have changed from his school clothes, she thought. She'd never seen him in his St. Mark's private-school uniform. She saw some dark material bunched in a corner. Maybe the uniform. Ceci wondered if this was one of the days they wore ties. Every day but one. Which? Friday? He was saying something about a moratorium. Sounded like natatorium. Auditorium. Black armbands, he said. The TV was saying, Allison said she wanted peace; she said this to her mother on the phone yesterday. Tears on faces. Weeping. Gasps. Tear gas, said a man.

She wondered what the burn of tear gas was like. Pneumonia was a cold, rattly feeling. Did the tear gas burn your bronchial tubes forever down to the alveoli, something no machine could fix? Would it give you emphysema? She took a deep breath to remind herself that she was in good shape. I'm in good shape, she said to herself. My lungs are my friends. She listened to her breath, she felt the little bruise of pain at the end of each long breath, as always.

Look, he said, unfolding a letter from the envelope. Harvard wrote me and said fuck off.

For a moment she believed him and wondered at this disregard. Didn't they expect parents to read it? He unfolded the letter and read: Dear Mr. Schwartz, Unfortunately we cannot accept you for admission into Harvard College. We had many qualified candidates and we regret that we could not accept all of them. Our waiting list is filled, also, but we wish you success and achievement in your academic career and in the world beyond.

There's nothing I can do, he said. Nothing. He was down now, head on her shoulder like a baby, like a puppy. She touched his hair. She had never touched a boy's hair. Her father's hair was thinning, wet with Vitalis. This was poodle hair, like her own. She massaged his head, and with the other hand rubbed her own scalp, to feel what it felt like.

A kind of tickle. More exciting when it's two.

But not the kind of tickle that made her feel like laughing.

Then he was rocking and then he smashed his body against hers. My ribs, she thought. His ribs. Tackling. I'm a football player. My lungs are strong and fine. Maybe I will outgrow this asthma business after all. He held her in a bear hug. She had danced the bear hug three times at two different parties at the JCC and at Westwood Country Club. She pressed her lips against his face. Her mouth. Little scratchiness: he shaves! She wondered if he'd been crying, inched out her tongue. Salt.

He tongued her ear.

She tongued his. More like dirt than wax.

He cupped her chin.

Sweet Indian princess. She clamped her thighs. For no reason. And again. Again. She could feel his fingers all up and down her back almost like a massage. Or how she imagined a massage.

She clamped her thighs.

He moved his hands back to her face, made circles on her cheeks with his hands.

She rocked and rocked, the Indian princess. He was a puppy and so was she. Boys weren't like cats at all. I am not thinking, she was thinking. This is what it's like not to be thinking. Though if she was thinking this, she must be . . .

Puppy hair, puppy tail, knobs, elbows, salt. The boys didn't want to go, Allison said, the people were telling the microphone on TV. The boys didn't want to go. Poor poor thing, she was thinking. Poor thing, poor little puppyface, poor boy but so old he can drive, two-four-six-eight, don't give a damn, next stop—

My poor poor little beagle, she thought. Ceci, he whispered, Ceci honey, he whispered.

Ceci honey, she thought. I'm a honey. I'm Ceci honey. God please, she was praying rocking crying too, please God don't let him call me sweetheart.

# Liberator

My father was a liberator. I don't know when I first knew that. It's one of those things you know before you know what it means: My father was a liberator.

When he was a young man, a son, before he became a husband, father, owner of a Texas delicatessen, before he rejoined the family bubble-bath business, before his hair turned gray and thin, he was a member of a platoon that opened the gates of Mauthausen, the gates that his country would not bomb. Opened life back up, offered it to the prisoners, the ones who waited at the gates and the ones who did not wait.

He wore a dull uniform pinned with shiny badges, and shoes that glistened with mud. He was a liberator. Like a gladiator. Like a knight, his mail glinting in the sunshine, silvery as fish scales. I imagine him strong, sword upraised, a shield in the other hand. The frail grateful, kneeling at his feet. Like certain engravings of Lincoln with the slaves. Chains broken and rendered harmless, like beheaded snakes.

He loved Lincoln. Abraham, patriarch of a divided nation. Abraham, dark bearded like a Jew.

My father talks about Lincoln. He talks more about Lincoln than he talks about the war. A little bronze bust of Lincoln sits on the piano. As if he were a bringer of music. On the shelf, as far back as I can remember: Sandburg's biography. My father refused to read Gore Vidal's novel. He said, "Let an old man keep his illusions, Ceci."

But he is not an old man. He is a gray-haired, clean-shaven man who admires Lincoln. Some of the time he can remember who he was.

My father never signed up for an army reunion. He didn't tell war stories. He left Europe with the rest of the U.S. troops and went back to Houston, returned to work in his father's bubble-bath factory downtown. He stayed there for a year. Then he bought a delicatessen nearby. Named it Ruben Rubin's Reubens. He thought about making it kosher, decided that his clientele wouldn't care.

He was right. He patented his special five-course meal: peanuts in the shell, Lone Star beer, kosher-style Reuben sandwich, scoop of Borden's Butter Brickle, a Lovera cigar. His logo, on napkins, giveaway pens, plastic cups: a map of Texas, a corned-beef sandwich instead of a dot for Houston.

"A five-course meal," he says now. "I used to charge only a buck fifty. Can you believe it? In 1940s, 1950s dollars. The things you could buy for a dollar then. When a cup of coffee was really only a dime, just like in the songs."

I am here only for a visit, but he speaks as if I have always been here. Then other times, other times—I wait for those times, am relieved when they finally arrive: the worst, the mind like a naked wall, awaiting the family movies. "Who is it? Ruthie? Ellen? Miriam?"

Every time he looked out the window of the deli he could see the family bubble-bath factory, just down Main Street. On top of the factory was the Kewpie doll he'd designed as the symbol of Barnston's Bubblers just before the war. Dolly, the Barnston Bubble Girl. (My grandfather Chaim was the one who'd invented the name Barnston. Thought it sounded American, New Englandy. Instead, it sounded like an Ellis Island name. Suppliers would call the factory, demanding to speak with Bernstein, the owner.) Every day from the deli window, my father would watch Dolly twirling in neon, and every Friday he would take my mother to his parents' house for Shabbat dinner. And every Shabbat my grandfather would wink at them and say, "You know what they say, Ruben, Ruthie—the Sabbath is the time to be fruitful and multiply."

That part I do not know for certain. I am spinning here. I know that for six years my parents were not fruitful; they were fruitless, nonmultipliers. They did not divide, add, or subtract. I imagine my grandfather, for whom I am named (Chaim becoming Charles, becoming Chaya, my Hebrew name, turning into Cecilia, Ceci), leaning over my grandmother's white tablecloth, the one she would soak in bleach every Monday and hang out to dry; I see my not-yet-dead grandfather leaning his arm over the crumbs from the challah and asking, every Friday night, without fail: "When will you kids give us a grandchild? You know what the rabbis say about creating on the Sabbath—." I stop here, with the yellow crumbs making indentations on Chaim's lower arm, his fingers (long and sure, like my father's? like mine?) clasping my mother's, and my mother, circumspect, looking down, wanting to get up to help her mother-in-law in the kitchen, where she can hear water running over the china and silver. I stop with my mother's embarrassment, my father's slight dip into anger, wearying of his father's joke that never varies. I stop—it doesn't pay to delve too deeply into the lives of your parents. This is what I do know: My mother and father wanted children so badly that they consulted a specialist. He advised them to keep track of my mother's temperature every day. My older sister, Ellen, was a wanted child. This is what they told me once. Faces aglow. They didn't mean to tell, as if they felt a taboo against discussing someone else's wantedness.

In their sixth year of marriage, this is what did or did not happen. My father tells me this story on this visit. As if it is a parting gift. His speech is clear, like a polished window. I see the images perfectly, the way I see the entrance of the camps, the big iron gates, the dark, squalid barracks.

This is what he, Ruben, ex-liberator, ex-owner of a Texas delicatessen, ex-executive of a bubble-bath business, tells his daughter in English, his mother tongue: that one afternoon, after the press of the lunch crowd had ended in the deli, a man walked in. Quietly. "He had a scrunched-in face—like a crumpled piece of paper," says my father, scrunching up his face. The man was carrying a rolled-up Yiddish newspaper in his coat pocket. He must be visiting from New York, my father thought, must be in for Passover; hardly anybody in Houston read Yiddish newspapers. My father was intrigued by this man. He wanted to ask him how he came to be carrying a Yiddish paper, how he had happened upon Ruben Rubin's Reubens nonkosher deli in the heart of downtown Houston. It was the afternoon of the first night of Passover. Without thinking it through, my father asked him to the seder. It was going to be a small one—just my father, my mother, an engineering student from Rice, and his wife and three-year-old daughter. My grandparents had gone to Corpus Christi to be with elderly cousins. The real reason they left: My father had made it clear he needed to make his own table, away from pointed comments about where was a young child who could ask the Four Questions.

He called my mother to set another place. She was worried about having enough food. My father told her, "He's just a little old man. Very little." My mother laughed into the telephone. "I'll put more water in the soup," she said. I have heard her say this. She would say it when I brought friends home for dinner in junior high, and I would say, "What soup? Are we having soup?" My father said, "I'll bring him home with me." The man seemed content with the invitation, but not so grateful once he arrived at the house. He seemed to be a scholar. He knew much Hebrew and extemporized from the little Haggadahs that each person had, the Passover booklets that came free from Maxwell House coffee. He complained about the thinness of the service. Everyone grew tired, impatient, but he was from Europe, it was clear, and was therefore somewhat exalted.

Toward the end of the meal, my father asked the daughter of the engineering student if she would walk to the front door to open it for Elijah the prophet. "A cute kid," says my father now. "All red hair and freckles. They called her Howdy Doody for a nickname." The mother and daughter opened the door. The mother came right back to the table. The little girl dawdled. "I figured it's because her legs were shorter," says my father. As soon as she returned to the table, she started to cry.

"Blood streamed from her eyes." My father repeats this. Blood. He raises his eyebrows, impressed with the simplicity of this extraordinary sentence. "Real blood, Ceci," he says, looking straight at me. "I was thinking at the time, As if from a gunshot wound." Everyone saw this, her cheeks as if washed with dark red watercolor. But when they went to wipe it, the tears became transparent again, plain salt water, no stain on the napkin. He shakes his head. "The darnedest thing," he says. "It seems impossible. All we could do was stare."

And then the man, the strange little man, like a Yiddishe Rumpelstiltskin, carefully removed his shoes and climbed up onto his chair. He pointed his finger at my father and began to speak. His words were clumsy, dense, the words of a foreigner struggling for elevation: "You, Ruben of the double name, you Ruben, born of American soil, you looked at death in the eyeballs, you, you—," and then the rest of his words were in Yiddish, but a Yiddish no one could understand. Says my father, "A meshuggah kind of Yiddish, garbled, half words, pieces of words stuck on other words that didn't make any kind of sense. And I know my Yiddish, Ceci. I used to speak it like a native." He laughs, his old joke, because Yiddish is from no country, every country. "Your mother thought we should call the cops. I said, 'For what? Speaking a foreign language in America? Relax,' I told her. 'Have a good time. Bring on the dessert.' It was that coconut cake that she made every Passover, a recipe she got from Mother. I told her I'd make sure the old man didn't break anything." My father's eyes look to the side, as if seeing the same younger self that the old man saw. I have disappeared. I am not yet born.

My father continues: "And then the man kissed the little red-haired girl, who was now sleeping, and walked out the door that they had opened for Elijah. His kiss made a red mark right on her cheek. And that mark," says my father, pausing for drama, "that red mark, has confounded dermatologists to this day."

Where did the girl go? What is her name?

How, I wonder, did her parents explain the mark to her?

She would be eight years older than I am. I imagine myself searching the city for women with this mark, women with the Howdy Doody hair and freckles. I will not be distracted by marks on arms, legs, fingers. I will not imagine that her father left town as soon as he was awarded his engineering degree, that she has moved, had cosmetic surgery, or died.

That Passover night was the night they conceived my sister, Ellen. (I feel their tiredness, after the guests have gone. I see them washing and wiping the dishes, sweeping the floor. Or did my father say, "Ruthie, let the dishes go hang, we'll make a child, and if we like her, we'll make another." I see them clutching, clinging, into the night.) He puts it delicately: "That night we created your sister, Ellen." He looks down shyly. I count the months: April, May, June, July, August, September, October, November, December.

"Every day in life is a miracle, Ceci," he says, as if this is the logical end of the story, the story of the Mysterious Little Old Man Who Came to the Seder and Removed the Curse of Sterility. The story blossoms out of what is known as a lucid moment. Or more precisely, lucid passage of time. *Lucid*—a word no one uses except in cases like this.

When he is not lucid, I learn formulas for bubble bath, old marketing approaches abandoned, names of scented flowers, suppliers of corned beef. Shelf lives of fragrances. I hear what I think are Zionist Labor songs in Yiddish, which he must have learned from his father.

Sometimes he falls asleep in the middle. Drops off, head drooping on a pillow. In sleep he appears scholarly.

I ask my mother about the old man and she says, "Yes, there was a man—"

My father walks into the room, drowsily adds, "Like one of those St. Patrick's Day, St. Pat's—leprechauns."

He retrieves the word himself.

"—a funny little man," says my mother. (It hurts her to look at my father, to remember, actually hurts the most when he is silent, because then she forgets, forgets he has changed.) "I think he stole something," she says, "some little knickknack. Where did he come from? We never saw him again, did we? I think that couple brought him. What was their name? They both taught French, didn't they, at a high school in Clear Lake?"

"No, no," says my father, angry, and his face crumples up like paper.

I look for tears in the edges of his eyes.

"They had a daughter," I say. "With red hair. Maybe freckles."

My mother shakes her head. "No. There wasn't a child at either of the seders that year. Those were the smallest seders we've ever had. That was the year Chaim and Rose went to Corpus. There was only that couple and the old man. I remember I had to ask the Four Questions. I sang it with that French woman. She was French or Belgian. I think she was Belgian, yes, she was Belgian, I remember thinking I'd never met anybody from Belgium before. I kept thinking about lace. She'd met her husband in Europe, during the war. He was American, and he spoke French, and she spoke beautiful English. I remember the tunes were the same. I couldn't get over that, that she'd learned the same tunes for all the prayers in Belgium. It gave me the shivers." Goose bumps rise on her arms, now. "The next year, that was the year Ellen was a baby, and Chaim took pictures all during dinner."

What about the little man?

"He just up and left in the middle of everything," she says. "Why—?" She is going to say, Why bring it up now? Then she remembers again that she is grateful for any link he can give her, any bridge to the past life they had, because it makes him closer, but then she remembers the closer he is, the more painful it all seems. She sighs, turns away.

Then, in a minute, two, the scrim drops and he asks, "What man? What man? What little man?"

He does not look different. He does not, for example, drool. He has his teeth. He does not gum. He looks the same.

They still sleep in the same bed, together; he's on the left, she's on the right. Which gates, once opened, remain open?

My father was a liberator. This is undeniable. There are records that declare it. They are in books, on microfilm, on microfiche, in government depositories, in archives. You can look up ranks, platoons, serial numbers. Combat Command B of the Eleventh Armored Division of the Third Army. You can watch documentaries, read diaries and memoirs of survivors and soldiers and workers from the Red Cross. You can examine maps, store up details, memorize the lexicon. Kapos. Badeanstalten. Mussulmen. Mussulmen were the slaves who lost all hope, who moved like zombies. Became as foreign and unknowable as Moslems. Named for the hollow-eyed people seen in newsreels, before the war, starving in foreign lands.

My father and his buddies in Combat Command B opened the doors of Mauthausen, eighty miles from Vienna, and liberated the people who might have been us, the people we used to be. They were emaciated, diseased. Some were too frightened to come out of their shacks. Some gathered a minyan and prayed. Some stooped down to kiss American hands and feet.

My father was a liberator. He roams the neighborhood. He talks about Lincoln. He takes bubble baths. He eats corned-beef sandwiches. There are times he remembers how much he has forgotten.

And times that he remembers only that he's forgotten. And times that he says, "What little old man? What delicatessen? I was never a soldier boy, soldier boy. I was killed in the war. A bullet pierced my skull. All men are created equal. God sails the open seas."

The books about the liberators say that most of them are silent about the experience. Even the ones who are Jewish. An alloy of pride, impotence, fragility. I get this idea and I fight it: that a piece of shrapnel of the past is lodged in his brain, damming up the currents of now, of this life, and if he could remove it—if I could remove it—his life would come flooding back to him.

Or this: If he could somehow retrieve the crazy, garbled Yiddish words of the old man, unravel the riddle of the Rumpelstiltskin, and get them translated—find some combination scholar-psychiatrist, a healer, who could tell us what the message was that the old man was trying to impart—.

When my father arrived at Mauthausen on May 5, 1945, I imagine he felt mingled pity, grief, shame: They did this to his people. But they were not his. His people were the men in his division, men who were dressed like he was, in drab, helmeted to protect themselves. They shared coffee, cigarettes, they joked. The ones from the South had familiar accents. They passed around pictures of their girls, of Betty Grable. They were fighting for those legs. For Veronica Lake's curtain of hair.

The story is: We always arrive too late, never knowing what the other has seen. We open gates that others have locked. Scraping the earth as we pull. Rooting out grasses tethered, clinging.

He did or did not tell the prisoners he was Jewish. Is it too much to say that he saw his own death there?
Probably.

Did you try to use Yiddish? Did you look for those who could understand English? Did you ask them, as the doctor asks you, "What is your name? What is your family name? Where are you from?

How old are you? Are you in pain? Do you know what is wrong?" Did you ask them in Yiddish, the language of your early lullabies and curses: "Brothers, sisters, where did your lives go? At what point did you feel it fly from you? Did you strain to catch it? Did you shrug, did you turn away?"

# Pageant

Ceci Rubin's mother has driven her from Houston to San Antonio for a talent show. It is a Saturday. Usually Ceci spends her weekends at charm-school classes for little girls at Neiman's and acting lessons at the Alley Theater's children's school. When she misses class for a contest, she makes up the work on weeknights. Her mother helps her with this juggling and preparing—she is Ceci's "aide de crimp," her father once said, and Ceci parrots the phrase. Her mother has helped her, for example, incorporate her eyeglasses into her act. She has learned to remove them and gesture at appropriate spots, so that now they seem necessary to her performance—"Absolutely indispensable," as Ceci puts it. It is eleven-thirty, and they have just arrived at the parking lot of San Antonio High School. The humid air disappoints—her mother had promised it would be dry, after all they were going west, even if it was along a river. She fears her curls will turn to frizz.

In the middle of the stage of the Davy Crockett Auditorium, Ceci does her act—her little elocution, Kay Thompson's Eloise. ("I am Eloise. I am six. I am a city child. I live at the Plaza. . . .") Though Ceci has no experience of New York or the Plaza, her idea of New York is so strong that it wouldn't matter if New York were mythical. She speaks of the historic New York that drew James Thurber and, in the very same tradition, Garrison Keillor. She does not know of Garrison Keillor yet. No one does. Ceci is eight and pouty lipped and does not yet have the feeling, Who are you to thrust yourself in the public eye? She is judged a finalist, but she does not win. She is in the top four. She has come to expect this. She hardly ever wins. When she does, she is confounded, does not know how to react. Grace does not come naturally to her.

Her grandparents have driven in from Austin. They have brought flowers. She has always wanted roses, white roses. She thinks roses are elegant. Grandma and Grandpa have brought her purple irises from the garden. They are wrapped in paper towels and foil. They have held them throughout the performance, or maybe left them sitting on a chair. The edge of one petal is wet and crinkled and dark like lettuce gets when it's handled too much. It is ruined. They have brought her garden flowers ruined by their lack of care. And she has lost.

"The judges did not understand," says her mother; "they are too Texan." Her mother is trying to thank her parents for Ceci. For coming out. Ceci does not thank them. She wants them to take her to an elegant French restaurant (the type that Eloise eats in, Ceci imagines), and if they cannot buy her a whole bouquet, she wants one perfect white rose at her place, next to the dinner napkin rolled in its silver holder. She wants them to ask her opinion of the dumb singer from Kerrville and her "Nearer My God to Thee." Ceci is eight but she has heard about the separation of church and state. Her father talks about it. He has explained it to her. She wants to know if the girl can be arrested for singing about a Christian God in front of all of them, this Saturday afternoon of Ceci's Sabbath, when her grandparents usually go to services and eat herring and *kichel* and talk to their friends.

She has seen her grandfather pray. He stands and makes a great noise. It is embarrassing. He vibrates like the windup organ grinder and monkey Ceci has at home. She does not know these people—her mother's parents—well at all. Sometimes she feels she is an orphan. She has imagined the orphanage she came from, a place like Madeline lives in with Miss Clavel.

Her mother gives her a slight shove, says, "Thank your grandparents for the flowers." She wants to kick them. She wants to wake them up from thinking she is merely an eight-year-old produced by their daughter and son-in-law Ruben, a little girl who does not understand life. She understands life. She talks to God. She talks to her dog. She understands the pain of asthma. She has been to deep places but she cannot begin to find the words to tell them this. She too wonders about suffering. She has read the diary of Anne Frank, slowly, carefully, because the style is too old for her. Like the dresses she sometimes wears. When she dresses up she looks like she's going to a job interview.

She is very young. She is only now learning how to write in cursive. Her classmates make fun of her special trips but are awed by the prizes and clippings she brings to Show-and-Tell. (She is still that young, to have a Show-and-Tell.) They are standing here forever, these three generations, between the first row and the stage. All around, other families are talking, the shurring and hissing that has become so familiar—the crying of the poor losers, sore losers—and the smell of sweat mixed with the sticky fragrances of the sponsors: sulphury hair perm, strawberry perfume for girls, ubiquitous cloying junior hairspray. The sweet sure smell of red lipstick. (White lipstick smells different, more waxy, more like chocolate.) The crayon smell of the eyebrow pencil. Ceci's mother doesn't let her wear more than a dash of eyebrow pencil under and along her eyelashes, but other girls wear layers of mascara, acres of it, false eyelashes, even, glittery eyeshadow. Sometimes she borrows blue-violet eyeshadow from a girl from Bastrop who shows up at all the same competitions, and she puts a dab on the corner of her eyes. It is the color of the irises plucked from her grandparents' yard.

Her grandparents are standing right in front of her. She faces them, the way she did when she was onstage. They are impatient. They are more disappointed than she is. They wanted their large, awkward daughter to have produced cuddly grandchildren. They want Ceci to be cute and Kewpie lipped, a delightful child who would wow the judges, and here they have this sullen unappreciative thing who didn't even win a ribbon. Who wants to be consulted on theological matters, though they do not know this. She cannot tell them, cannot tell them how she spends time wondering if Joseph in the Bible—that is what she calls him, out of some sort of respect, Joseph-in-the-Bible—brought his fate upon himself. She feels a kinship with him, feels his joy at the flamboyant coat, his pain in the pit, alone, such fear, such casting out. She doesn't tell them any of this. Years later, she imagines them saying, "Why didn't you tell us what you were feeling?" And she imagines answering, accusing, "Why didn't you?" But by the time there is peace, it is too late, they have grown feeble, and when she is in her twenties, when she asks her grandmother questions, the older woman recoils: "Why do you come here and ask and ask?"

But back then, time is stretching out and they are standing there forever and Ceci is silent. Her grandmother with her cracky voice (it has been that way for years and years, forever) says, "Well, Ceci, it's not the end of the world, we thought you did very well," and Ceci hears the patronizing tone in her grandmother's voice, though she doesn't have that word yet. She hears the separation, what lies beneath it: I am old and know much and you are my daughter's child, two generations removed, you will never know what we know, and she hears in that voice, You are not as good as we are, and the tragedy of the misunderstanding grips her, though she does not know this is what it is.

They do not understand, the judges do not understand, and for the first time Ceci becomes dissatisfied with Eloise, because Eloise cannot help her now—this flimsy Eloise, this Curious George in skirts, who cannot look at the deeper questions, who cannot lead her to words that reach into the audience and grab souls. Ceci desperately wants to make a difference in their lives. She does not want her grandparents' irises-picked-from-the-yard because they don't make her feel special enough and she wants to shock them with her erudition or her melodrama but cannot. I am not who you think I am. She is only half their size and dressed like Eloise in a dark pleated skirt, white blouse, and a red bow in her hair. She is determined to bite her mother's parents if they say she looks cute.

She doesn't answer them. She feels badness swelling inside her. She doesn't want their damn flowers. She is frightened of saying this word in front of them. She takes the flowers and drops them and for a moment she still has a chance—she could pick them up, say the minimum: "Thank you" or "Sorry." But she doesn't. She won't. If they were to take her to the guillotine she would not say them.

A beat. She steps on the flowers—she grinds the purple loving-hands-from-home irises with the toes and heels of both of her dull black leather Mary Janes. She imagines the flower juice coming up through the soles to make her legs stronger and stronger to push down even more. To kill every ounce of the flowers. Her grandmother flutters: "Oh Cecilia, you're just disappointed in losing. You still deserve flowers." She moves to pat her head.

But Ceci's mother knows better. Ceci's mother knows of her badness. She grabs Ceci's arm, and a feeling of danger that is almost sexual, that is sexual, rises in Ceci. She knows what her mother will do—

she fears, she hates her mother and everyone else at this moment. Ceci the Stuckup Snob (as they call her at these contests, a few of the girls, just a few) will get her comeuppance in front of the little girls who cry when they lose, Ceci who never cries in front of anyone for any reason, who says, "I don't care so much; I do it for the experience."

Ceci's mother is grabbing her, in anger, in her shame before her own parents, shame that she has raised her daughter wrong, has made all the wrong decisions, ended up with the wrong family, a family that is not the way she wants it to be. Her husband, Ruben, makes bubble bath for the fun of the nation, so he says, but is too tired after supper to do anything but play solitaire and watch TV, and has not danced with her, for example, since their own wedding. Her other daughter, who is not in contests, stays home quietly and does not misbehave, but is so private that she might as well be a boarder. Ceci's grandparents have accused Ceci's mother of pushing her, Ceci has heard them say that, they have said she is living her dreams of glamour through this poor child, and once they even ventured to say she could be causing her daughter's asthma.

Now Ceci's mother has wrenched her across her lap and the mother's frustration pounds into the daughter, sharp surprise cracks of pain, real pain, that should not be surprises because she's felt them before, she expects them, maybe she even deserves them, like her mother tells her. They sting, they push her hips into her mother's legs, they make noise louder than the pain, and all Ceci can feel is she hates her she hates her, she wants her to die. Ceci knows she could lie here face down and be perfectly still, like a European martyr, but instead she screams without words, even though she knows its fuels her mother's anger and will make her attack go on forever, and Ceci digs her pink-painted fingernails into her mother's calves, and their bodies are locked in battle, with a ferocity that can't let up.

It is finally her grandfather who tears them apart.

Ceci cannot imagine how she will ride back four hours with this woman who wants to kill her. She runs through a doorway back to the school gym just down the hall. Each of the girls had been assigned a locker there. She undresses in the shower stall so no one will see as she sheds her underwear. She turns, while the water is running, touching the redness of her bottom, the way her sister showed her with sunburn: touch it, turns white, lift finger, turns red again. She stays under the shower forever it seems, the water running hot and strong over her sticky hairsprayed hair and down to her bottom, where it still hurts. She soaps it over and over and listens in awe to the depth of her own sobbing, gasping into hiccups, her lungs still clear, and then starts to sing, to replace the wordless breaths, a mix of everything: "Hatikva," "Dead Man's Curve," "Go Away Little Girl," "David Melech Yisrael," and finally turns off the water, fascinated by the white wrinkles of her fingers, almost transparent on the tips. She imagines they will never be restored to smoothness.

In the car Ceci gets in the backseat to punish her mother, saying she wants to stretch out and sleep. Her mother plays news radio, switching from town to town. The same sentences, different voices.

At home Ceci does not, as she usually does, go running to her father.

Time passes. Ceci enters more competitions. But she is changed. She looks for serious parts and is named a finalist fewer and fewer times. "Whatever can that girl's mother be thinking of?" the judges wonder. Sometimes the judges do take a liking to her, the very few who actually enjoy the idea of a nine- or ten-year-old reciting the memoirs of Eleanor Roosevelt and Helen Keller. But Ceci's career on the talent circuit quickly winds down.

Later she will mark that afternoon in San Antonio High as not the end of her childhood or of anything hallowed like innocence but the day she realized that no one understood her, no one would ever understand her, the day she felt her heart begin to close. As years went by, even as she refused to confide in him out of a sense of loyalty to her mother, whose disappointment she sensed and somehow took as her own fate, Ceci wanted more and more to become her father Ruben—safe in his office with consumer surveys and marketing plans, reports of chemical analyses and European breakthroughs, where nothing of this life could touch him.

# Brunch

When Bruce has brunch, he makes two trips to the Jewel, then sits at his beat-up table and tells me, "Ceci, there are no happy couples, only people who haven't broken up yet." Then he jumps up to check the Nicaraguan drip-grind decaf and runs back to the store and thinks up puns about lox. When Bruce makes brunch, he could invite Barry, but he can't invite Barry if he invites me, because since we broke up, I won't see Barry. And Bruce has to give me first dibs on all invitations, because I've known him since before we knew anybody else. Bruce and I met at O'Hare, first day in town for both of us. He doesn't even ask if he can invite Barry. He knows. And if he did ask, I'd turn around and say, "If I had a brunch, could I invite Sally?" Only it's not the same because since March, Sally's been living in D.C.

Now Bruce is planning a brunch and I ask if Sam's coming. Bruce says no, that he's got that conference in Carolina on religion and the left, and he'll be back Monday. Bruce doesn't know about Sam and me. If Sam came to brunch, I wouldn't leave, but we'd probably try to ignore each other at first, then talk a little too loud, and laugh a little too hard, and lecture a little too much, and finally have a tight, whispered conversation in the kitchen. We'd tell people we were talking strategy.

Most of us met through coalitions. Bruce knows Barry from the fight against Contra aid. Bruce was a liaison to the Quakers. Barry was a liaison from the Quakers. The first time Barry said he loved me was at a conference on the sanctuary movement. When we broke off, I said, "You take the Religious Task Force, I'll take Fellowship of Reconciliation." When Bruce and Sally broke up, they were working on Harold Washington's election out of the North Side campaign office. Sally moved down to the South Side office. She refused to help at a training session for deputy voter registrars because she knew Bruce and his friends would be running it. She voted absentee so she wouldn't see anybody she knew at the polling place.

With each breakup, our territories get smaller and smaller. I do solidarity work with Central American labor unions, but now only ones in Guatemala and Honduras. When Barry and I broke up, he refused to give up El Salvador. He writes to the FDR leaders in Spanish. In his Spanish for Progressives class, he met Brenda. She runs a Third World trading outfit and used to live with Ben. They met on Washington's first campaign for mayor. They believe that monogamy is bourgeois. I think she and Barry sleep together occasionally. I don't think either removes their woven "friendship" bracelets for the disappeared in Guatemala. I don't take mine off when I sleep. No one was wearing them back when I first met Bruce. The disappeared weren't disappeared yet, or we didn't know yet, word hadn't filtered back to us. Sally used to wear hers even when we went swimming. Barry had his before I met him. I think some Buddhists gave it to him when he protested at the UN.

In the middle of the old days, Barry and I would have brunch and invite Bruce, Sally, Brenda, Ben, Alan, Helen, Art, Crista, Mark, Esther, Liz, Frank. We didn't hang out with Sam. Now Crista and Art are divorced. Liz and Frank are engaged. Brenda and Ben are an occasional. The rest aren't speaking. Barry has my skis and skates and on the phone we discuss his returning them, in exchange for his socks and second-best tennis racket. He gets mad because I won't talk with him about these in person.

So I don't make brunch.

Once there was a time when I didn't know all of them. But I hardly remember it. I get calls from that time. From Ajax. He's out in California making bookcases. I wait for him to want me back. He tells me about his kids. I know you can't erase kids.

Barry doesn't want me back. Bruce doesn't want Sally back. Crista doesn't want Art back. Helen doesn't want Alan back. Mark wants Esther back but is too proud to say so. Brenda and Ben still talk free love. On weekends I see Crista and Alan and Tom or Art and Jan and Esther, but never Crista and Art or Jan and Alan or Helen. We can't go to anyone's old favorite restaurants, so we go to new places no one likes all that much. Before fund-raisers, we make extensive calls to determine who'll be there.

On the El I think: I will see someone I know. Or, That man over there will fall for me. Barry sees Sam on the El. They talk baseball and nerve-gas legislation.

On weekends, Barry goes camping in Michigan. He doesn't take anyone to his fund-raising dinners, doesn't mention my name anymore at work, doesn't have anyone to call My Little June Bug.

I don't know why he started calling me that. He'd write it on letters, say it into my answering machine, buy me bugs made of licorice or chocolate. He'd send me cards showing sweet domestic scenes in color on the front, and inside, on the blank part, he'd write: "To my one, my only, Bed Bug."

On weekends, I call Sally in Washington or she calls me. We talk about Bruce. I don't tell her about Sam and me: Three weeks. Three Saturday nights ago, after the benefit at the Heartland Café for Nicaraguan medical aid. Weather a bit warmer than tonight, even. We were sitting on Sam's porch. I said, "It's nice out here." Sam said, "You're pretty." He said, "You fascinate me." He twirled the curls at the back of my neck. He frightened me. Fascination, I thought. Awe. I can't live with awe. But I did. I hung in. Two weeks later, he said: "I bit off too much. I confess. I hadn't expected—." He said, "It's not the right time."

I am not the right person at the right time. I was not the right person for Sam, Barry, Theo, or Helen. Tom and Ajax were not the right people for me. Sally was not the right person for Bruce.

I am twenty-nine. Helen is twenty-eight. Bruce is thirty-two and has worked in three presidential campaigns. Sally is twenty-eight. Barry and Theo are both thirty. Sam is thirty-four. Ben is thirty-five. Brenda's thirty-one. Crista is twenty-seven. Art is forty. Mark is thirty-five. Esther is thirty. Liz is thirty-four. Tom is thirty-five. Michael the sculptor is a month and a day younger than Sally. Ajax is thirty-eight. Bebe, his new girlfriend, is twenty.

Back when my sister Ellen and I were little, before either of us had ever had a boyfriend, we would ask each other, "If you had to marry somebody now, who would it be?"

Who would it be? Would it be Bruce, Sam, or Barry? Or Ajax? Or Tom? Maybe Sam, because it would be a challenge to make him grow to love me, like he said he did three Saturday nights ago. It's the challenge that people accept when they adopt a dog from the SPCA that's termed "a discipline problem," thinking, Not me, I'll be the one who tames it. Would it be Barry? No, because he would grow abrupt. He would be impatient and refuse counseling.

It was Sally who'd introduced me to Barry. She'd met him through Michael the sculptor, and she'd met Michael at a New Year's Eve party put on by Artists against Racism. When she came back to visit this summer, she showed me the house where the party had been. Or so she thought. She wasn't sure. She'd been drunk. Nine years before. Every time we passed a yellow Rabbit, she said, "I wonder if that's the car I sold when I left here."

Once I was going to be her maid of honor. She was going to marry Bruce. She bought a mid-calf-length tea dress, pinky peach, with lace. Then he decided he didn't want anything for life, though he still wanted to live with her. She left for six months and came back for two years before leaving for good. During that six months, she went around the world. One afternoon she was on a boat in Indonesia. She turned and saw a man sitting on a bench on deck in three-quarter profile. He looked like Michael—Michael, the sculptor from her early twenties, whom she'd met on New Year's and had left by May because he was jealous of her time. The man on the bench was asleep and he slept like Michael, head thrown back, arms out. Sally cried for two hours. When she describes this to me, her voice still breaks.

# Love

We are in love but you don't know it. You are slow on some of these ordinary things; you grow angry when I mention liberation theology, Adam Smith's unseen hand, proposals to ban land mines—things I thought everyone knew about, were in the atmosphere, but you are impervious to them, breathing your own mist. You think I am trying to show off. You know the Pre-Raphaelites and Sabbath prayers. We are in love but you don't know. I knew the moment I stepped into your old house to help you move. You were looking so young, like a teenager, in green, your hair held back in one of those oversized barrettes you wear, your face fresh scrubbed, innocent as a bobby-soxer. You had turned into someone else, someone small and unhoused. You were someone from the 1940s. I wanted to become a man, a tall dashing man. For the first time, I wanted another woman. I felt I should sweep you off your feet, put an arm around your back, dance with you. You told me which boxes to put in the car. You wrapped your pink azalea plant in your grandmother's quilt. You looked for your sleeveless down jacket. You couldn't find your Birkenstocks. I said I'd follow you, already sad at the thought of being separated for the fifteen miles into the city, wishing for the first time that we had CB radios. But I said nothing. You said, Ceci, come on, get in my car and I'll drive you back later. We were like cops on a mission. Partners.

We listened to the radio. We made five trips up the three flights of your new apartment, parking in back, walking through doors like medieval gates. At every turn, vistas like the ghetto, like the cobbled streets of Vilna neither of us has seen. You locked both doors, five locks in all. You put the pink azalea next to the window.

We drove to a café on Sheridan. I ordered potatoes and cheese, and you got an omelette. There was confusion over substitutions. We waited a half hour. When I was still eating, a big homeless man in plaids asked, Are you finished? I'm hungry. I said no. I gave him a dollar.

You treated. I said, You don't have to. You said, For helping me. I said, You'd help me. You said, That's the only reason people are helping me move, so I'll help them later. So don't pay, I said. You did anyway and I left the tip.

I cleaned my plate.

We unroll your futon and sit against the pillows. You change your shirt, walking around the room, talking. If you knew, you would be in the next room. In the bathroom. You don't know any lesbians. Once I told you I might go to their Sabbath services. You studiously ignored that.

You unwrap your framed print of Rossetti's *Beata Beatrix*. You lean it against the wall, next to the Burne-Jones. You cannot find your hammer. We have tea, the first tea in your new apartment. It is Russian, loose and black from a tin box, poured in tall glass mugs. In your old house, you'd cut up apples and place them on the bottom of the cup. Your pottery candlesticks are on the table, the ones I knew from your old kitchen. I am an old Jew, you say. We met among old Jews, the only people under fifty at a lecture on the origins of Yiddish. Evanston Library, middle of the day, what did I expect? Not that I would meet my true love, her red-brown Jewish hair streaming down her back in waves, her very serious dark eyes watching the speaker, her solemn face shifting to appreciate a joke. And soon you saved me, whisked me out of my Cinderella existence as a temp, got me an office next to yours at the community college, teaching English four days a week, half-paid-for insurance. Sometimes I feel we are as old as the rest of that library audience. It seems that no one our age keeps the holidays. You know an Israeli who asks you the date of Passover, asks why you light the candles, buy challah and wine. You don't like to answer. He's the one who told you about the vacant apartment in his building. We can see his kitchen table from across the courtyard. He is out. We can see a pot on the stove, a vase of yellow flowers.

Your family was famous. My cousin the genealogist said one of ours married one of yours. Your family produced Freud, Marx, famous rabbis that people have heard of. We are descended from someone out of favor with the Gaon of Vilna. Frequently in hiding, misplaced. There are stories of boats missed, visits to doomed towns.

My relatives were scholars manqués, artists manqués, poets manqués. My great-grandfather took an overdose during the Depression. His son studied law and was a genius designing ladies' hats. The other side of our family is known for producing high-quality bubble bath that many dermatologists recommend.

Now we have the same job, same title (ESL Instructor II), same size index card on each office door announcing our names and office hours. We have the same degree—bachelor of fine arts—and we both fell in love with the Pre-Raphaelites in college, you for the art, me for the politics. We say the same thing about our jobs: Good for now, it leaves us time for other things. Though we don't do the other things, which presumably would launch us into our real careers. We celebrate the same holidays, we both can read Hebrew. We are not observant to the same extent—I don't keep kosher. Neither of us knows Yiddish.

You lock the five locks and drive me back to my car. I imagine you like a painting. I cannot imagine being lost in your hair. I imagine you surrounded by flowers like Ophelia (alive), and our sharp small breaths.

I think of buying you tulips.

You say, Come visit always. You say, Parking's not that bad. You say, Come, we'll make a Sabbath.

Each morning at ten we talk on the phone. If we remember our dreams, we tell them. You dream me drowning in mud. You shouted and I said, Don't try, it's too hard. You went for help. You came back and I was on land, rescued by strangers. I dream we are entwined on the moon. But I don't say it. I dream we are in a Laundromat, yellow shag carpet. We are carrying bundles of warm clothes. They keep falling. The carpet is a meadow. There is a sun in each machine. Your clothes are the size of my hand. My clothes grow large, into sheets. We stretch out and fall asleep, our shoulders uncovered.

In our ESL classes, we talk to the students about their families. We hear of houses, guns, ghosts, rice fields, and open skies. I draw family trees on the blackboard. I teach them the word *deceased* and how to abbreviate it under a name. I explain that I'm from Poland and Russia. No, I say, not really me, my grandparents. I have not been there.

Where were your children born? asks Hua.

I do not have children, I say.

Americans are rich, says Jimei. Why they not like children? Teacher, you married? Teacher, why you not have children? You have brother, sister?

We make a Sabbath in your apartment. We are silent between the blessing of the wine and the bread—a ritual we learned from a book. We cover the bread—she is sensitive, says the story. She is sad the wine is blessed before she is, so we cover her ears. We talk about someday going to the lake first to greet the Sabbath Queen. We have heard too of *nefesh yesere*, the soul of the Sabbath that descends in peace. The old Jews of the Lower East Side saw it as the soul of socialism.

We pour sauce over pasta. I feel safe, I feel I belong here.

You talk of a man, his silences, his mystery consulting trips, the way he says your new apartment with its hardwood floors and second-hand furniture makes the new stereo look out of place. He has two sets of clothes for work—for the office and for the field, where he searches out toxic dumps. Can you see me with him? you ask. He is your size, has your wavy hair. He is always nervous, paces. When you went to the movies with him, he was too polite, held the door open for everyone. He quoted three different critics. Afterward you sat in his car and listened to an all-news station. He coughed and kissed you on the lips and coughed again.

Can I see him with you? What I don't see is how you could see yourself with him. What is there in him to draw you in?

We have dinner at your old friend Andy's. I meet his brother, and a week later when I sleep with him, you say, I didn't have that in mind at all. You think he's too thin, too unsubstantial. A *luftmensch*, a man who lives on air. His voice on the phone sounds like a wire. He reminds me, This is just casual. But he says he feels passion. I say I love him because it rolls from my mouth during sex. I say, Let's go to

Jamaica, one of those last-minute bargains. He says, There's not enough time. He dreams I send him postcards that say I'll love him forever. I send him blank cards with a note: Dreams don't mean.

You are glad when it ends. You say, You need someone with more bone and muscle.

We go to a café near school so often that we feel like regulars, but we don't look like most of the other clientele. We look soft and shabby next to the hard-edged punks who practically fill it up. They look like Death with their silver studs and black leather jackets and Cleopatra eyes. You hate them. I see them as perpetual trick-or-treaters. I don't tell you that I didn't look much different my last year of college. We look at a girl who has black hair with yellow roots, shaven strips above her ears. What if your child had hair like that? you ask. I wouldn't care, I say.

You wouldn't allow it. You say, I won't allow my children to play with yours. I say, I'm going to be the kind of mother that other kids will tell their mothers about. They'll say, But so-and-so's mother lets them sleep out in the backyard.

I have an image of myself in a pink-and-white-striped fifties dress of my mother's, red lipstick, and curly but controlled hair, tiptoeing to the lawn where my little darlings and their friends are giggling and playing old maid by the light of a flashlight. Motherhood is easy, I'm thinking. Left to their own devices, children will be good. That image fades into one of Ethel Rosenberg, same era, snapped in her kitchen, a dishrag hanging on the side of the frame.

America treats its people badly, I say.

What do you mean? you say.

It fries its dissidents.

How can you feel that way and teach people to be Americans? you ask.

This is old territory. I say as always that we're as American as anybody else. Who should be teaching immigrants? Some CEO?

And then you say, as always, Yeah, you're right, it could be worse, indicating them, shaking your head toward the sharp-edged kids at the next table. They could be the ones explaining citizenship and gerunds.

And what else should we do? A job is what I'm waiting for, a real job—a job that involves changing things. Like the world. As long as there's no lobbying or fund-raising. As long as it's something I believe in. Pure in its way.

And you, you want to teach people about art. Which means, practically speaking, grad school. Art history for you, journalism or politics for me. But not yet, we're still young.

With you, it's not like a constant buzz. It's not the brief heady rush with Andy's brother. But I imagine us in five years, ten years, sleeping together in a cozy apartment with hardwood floors and thick tapestries, pursuing our separate lives during the day, meeting after work in cafés such as this one, maybe even this one, at this table, in these chairs, repeating familiar patterns of conversation and argument, grown precious because so familiar, so dear.

You give yourself a birthday party. Your old lovers are there along with friends from high school, some people from work, from earlier jobs and the new neighborhood. I buy you cheesecake from the place the café buys it. Andy says, I'm her oldest friend. I think, But I know her the best. And through you and his brother I know all about him. I know about college road trips and about *Hiawatha*, which his father used to recite to put the kids to bed. I cut the cheesecake, and Andy serves it. Your eyes look black in the candlelight, you look like a Pre-Raphaelite in my present, a crown of dried flowers I bought at the Renaissance Faire. Everyone has given you things to wear. They are all golden and from other countries or eras: a tiny polished earcuff from Mexico, a small *chai* pendant, hoop earrings, an Indian scarf with bright threads. You are wearing them all and someone momentarily stuns us with a bright flashbulb. We are all your courtiers, bringing you offerings in candlelight and vanilla incense in an almost-safe urban neighborhood of new and old immigrants. We are adorning you like a tree, like a chorus in a school pageant on pluralism. I wonder what it is that makes people feel so proprietary. Are we creating you in our own image, are we feeding the image you have of yourself, do we see in you the golden dreams our grandfathers brought with them to America?

My great-grandmother, the story goes, came to America in 1920, alone. She was fifty-five. Took trains from Kiev to Ostend, a boat to New Orleans, a bus to Shreveport. We do not know what she ate along the way, whom she spoke to, whether she crocheted on the trip or attempted to learn English. She was a pigeon-faced woman who had lived for fifteen years on letters, written in Yiddish, from her sons in America. We do not have on record how she felt about the Revolution of 1905 or her preferences for the Bolsheviks or Mensheviks. We assume she knew enough Russian to communicate with the peasants who traded in the market once a week. We do not know how she chose or was chosen by her husband, or whether she fantasized, like Catherine the Great, about horses. Her name was Soreh-Leah. We do not know of any nicknames.

She met her daughters-in-law when they were already mothers. She could not speak to her grandchildren. She made tablecloths and bedspreads, sat on the porch out of the way of "the colored girl," reading month-old copies of the *Forverts*. She insisted the chickens in the backyard be slaughtered in the ritual manner. She said she wanted to die in the Old Country, her body cleansed in the town mikvah, wrapped in a shroud sewn by the burial society, and placed next to the remains of her husband, killed in a pogrom. In 1928 the whole family accompanied her to New Orleans, bearing bundles of cloth from their store, a box of elementary-school readers, and a copy of my grandfather's degree from the Louisiana School of Commerce and Industry.

My great-grandmother Soreh-Leah left America just before the Crash, never having seen the Grand Canyon, a sweatshop, or the Statue of Liberty. She did, however, says my father, take a great liking to baseball in the last few years and would go with the family to games of a St. Louis Cardinals' farm team, which had spring training in Shreveport.

In her later letters, she said Kishinev looked dry and brown after the tidy white clapboards and wild roses and sweet magnolia trees of Louisiana. Young people, she said, were studying in the gymnasia in Stalingrad and eating *traif* with the goyim. She missed the outings in the car for fresh ice cream straight from a local dairy, the bright colors the Negroes wore, and most of all, especially in winter, she missed the convenience of indoor, pull-chain plumbing.

My grandfather was a tailor and made ladies' clothing and hats. And what did your grandfather do?

My grandfather was a farmer. She killed in the war.

He. My grandfather he—I am thinking: The trouble is in Chinese there is no gender difference in the pronouns. I think of Spanish, where the gender of the possessive pronoun is determined by the object possessed. The object obsessed. Gender determines everything. Think of plumbing, electricity. Sockets, wires.

My grandmother is small. She pick fruit from the trees. I have picture. She make cakes for the children. It is sad.

Can you bring the picture tomorrow?

Will you be here tomorrow? If it's cold, they will be in class, in the junior college named for the disabled man who promised he would free everyone of the four fears. If it is warm, they will stay home with their children or walk to the lake. Will you be here tomorrow? Will you speak to me in your language until I understand everything, even what is not said? Is it possible to hear everything?

I have ticket from the photo shop. What is that, *color-process?*

*Process,* a way of making or doing something. What is the process for learning English? What is the process for registering for class? What is the process for getting your green card? What is the process for becoming a citizen?

And, Teacher, what is *proceed?*

*Proceed.* Proceed is to go forward. We will proceed to the next lesson. We will proceed until the bell rings for the break. We will proceed with our lives until the time comes for us to be cleansed and wrapped in our shrouds and placed next to our next of kin. When I bought my new wallet, it came with a card that said, In case of emergency call ————. I showed it to you and you wrote *God.*

We make a Sabbath. You've washed your floors, there's the slight scent of Murphy Oil Soap. Your floors are bright, reflect the candles. I've made the challah. We pull off hunks of it and add salt—a ritual we just read about—to make palpable the curse or prophecy: You will earn your bread by the sweat of your brow.

You praise my challah. It's thick, studded with golden raisins. I thought of you as I kneaded it, smoothed it with the heel of my hand, braided its ropes, brushed egg on the top so it would be brown and crunchy. Night is falling around us, and you've kept the lights down. I squint to make things even hazier. You look like me, I say. I always say this. No, you say, you look like me, which is what you always say. Is it the nose? I ask. Is it the eyes? you ask, or, Are it the eyes? Are it the ears? I ask. The hairs? you ask. The mouth? I ask. And then we drink more wine.

I go to Michigan for a weekend retreat on prayer and ritual, and when I come back, you've quit smoking and I've decided to keep kosher. Who knows, I say, maybe my hair will turn reddish and you'll start growing taller. Until we are twins, I think. Until we are the same. Today you'll have none of it.

Why are you like that? you ask. We aren't the same person. An echo of the elementary-school playground—She's copying us, she's trying to be like us.

We're in your apartment and the phone rings. I reach to pick it up. You take the receiver away.

I wasn't going to pretend to be you, I say.

I am reading about hidden homosexual couples. I read of Jane Addams. I know you have admired Jane Addams since third grade, but I don't tell you about this. You would say that some wishful lesbian was making it up for a dissertation topic, that lesbians can't imagine anyone living a life without sex. Or you would just say, Oh, in the noncommittal, disapproving way you have, and wait for the topic to finish itself off.

But I root for them, the way I felt happy for Eleanor Roosevelt when those erotic letters were published, even though everyone said it was just the conventional way women friends addressed one another. Because I would rather believe in lovesome and love-full than loveless, I cherish rumors of the secret lives of stern-faced reformers. Being happy in each other, we find everything easy, George Eliot wrote. About a man. About a gnomish man and she was a horseface of a woman. But to have that contentment to float on——.

Sometimes I get glimpses of it with you. Like odd sightings of God when edges of my disbelief burn off. But only glimpses. As if I'm on a tiny island and every so often notice the edge of a craft. No. As if I'm drifting on a raft and every so often look up and see the edge of something on the horizon. No, actually it's like being on the El, Howard Street line, and sometimes seeing, through short straight boulevards, through the trees, the lake flash in the sun. I know the lake's there but don't trust it not to disappear.

At the Art Institute is a painting by Anselm Kiefer called *The Order of Angels*. It is grainy and brown and black, like sandpainting. Metal strips lead from labels at the top—Cherubim, Seraphim, etc.—to mounds of brown and black swirls. In between is darkness that I think is the void but the guide says it is God. The big black bags are sacs where angels are made, factories going in spite of everything, small smoky fires after the Great Flood. And now I begin to understand: You have always believed in God. You trust the shadow voids on either side of Sheridan Road. I always want proof.

I decide I'm calling you too often, decide to wait for you to call first. Then you call. It's business. You ask me for authors your Level 5 students would understand. I say Hemingway and Zoshchenko and Judy Blume and then I feel you just called for that, using me for information, and I say, real snippy, Anything else? And you say, What's wrong with you? You say, You just asked me about library cards last week, you always make me feel like I'm wronging you, a criminal, I have to walk on eggshells. Fine, I say, if that's what you feel. I hang up, not reluctantly.

I unplug my phone for a week, and nod to you in the hallways. I realize it is easier than I thought not to run into you. I stay after class for long-needed student conferences.

At home, alone, I think of you. I think of love.

I love you because you said, after a dinner party at my apartment, that Diedre, my salamander, goes crazy when there are people in the room, she splashes and crawls up the sides of her bowl. I loved you for noticing.

I remember how last month I read in the paper a description of your neighborhood as a wild assortment of old Russian Jews, old Poles, Russian émigrés from the seventies, and young professionals. I called you because of the word *wild*. And then I asked, Has anything happened since we last talked? Which had been fifteen minutes before. You said, Oh, a lot.

I nearly believed you.

I love you because you still believe in God. Because in the times I do, I want to tell you. I don't believe in the liturgy; you don't believe in changing it or even getting rid of the pronoun so that it is never *he* but always God God God—or G———d, as you write it, the same way one of my students writes it. He is a Jew, the one Jew out of the wild assortment in the room.

Our first love, separately, was the Pre-Raphaelite movement. You showed me romantic paintings, Elizabeth Siddal and Janie Morris the models. I told you about Janie's husband, William, who tried to reform England by going back to medieval craftsmanship. I loved him for his energy. Because he tried to remake his country and spoke in long polite then torrential sentences about blackened skies and dehumanized men. Because he lashed out against imperialism. But Janie didn't love him. Because he was unkempt and distracted and had a big scratchy beard. Because he leapt out of bed at 5:00 A.M. to weave. Because he thought if you found the right recipe a whole new society would tumble into place. Because he loved her as the Ideal Woman and she did not see in him the Ideal Man.

Love was between the craftsman's fingers and the thread, in the shaping of the clay. Love was in the changing from sand to glass, love was the river of fire he went through that transformed him from bourgeois to socialist. Love was the eyes seeing what the clay could become, was in the idea of beauty everywhere, of useful delightful beauty, love was in reform.

The reason we don't love our jobs: because we imagine our students speaking like statesmen. We aren't mothers who love watching the process of learning, who delight in each new word. No, we want them to hatch full grown. We want more, we want gold and riches everywhere. We don't want to wait.

We want gold. We are greedy immigrants to this new land I can't find. We gobble all the seeds and end up with ground that lies fallow.

I decide to stop over, as if nothing has happened. You are doing laundry. I toss you warm clothes. I hold them against my cheek for one micromillisecond, thinking of my dream. What are you doing? you ask. Looking for a label, I say. I find the washing instructions. Obviously an import: Wash with cold water and snowflakes.

I toss it to you.


I bring a copy of my great-grandmother's picture to class.

Teacher, she leave and go visit and not come back?

Why she came to America if she leave? She go alone to Soviets?

Teacher, you desire memory?

I pass around the Xerox, a copy of the sepia print at home, where she stares, openmouthed, into the camera. She looks angry. I try to imagine her as a bush-baseball-league fan.

I say: In America, she went to baseball games. Have any of you seen baseball in Chicago? The Cubs, the White Sox?

This gets us through the rest of the afternoon. After class, you wait for me, we go to the café, unpack our papers, begin work. Like always.


We go back to the café the next day. We grade, talk, drink coffee, watch punks. Then we gather our papers from the table and put them in our Crate & Barrel bags (mine, gray; yours, tan). Our red pens go into the vinyl pen holders in the zippered front compartments. It's already dark. I'm filled with the froth of two double cappuccinos. We decide to walk partway along the lake. The moon is tangled among the branches of the three willow trees at Fargo Avenue. I stoop down for a handful of cold sand that feels like sugary snow. I say, Hold out your hand, and I sprinkle sand on your open palm. I grab—grasp— your hand. Listen, I say. My fingers brush the side of your face. They touch your earcuff. Could I go through with this? Now?

You wriggle your hand free. You turn your head.

That's all it takes.

We keep walking.

You ask if I'm sure it's too late to apply to teach summer school at the downtown campus. You tell me that your Israeli neighbor has bought health insurance for his cat. You tell me about the video that the Industrial Cooking Department offered to ESL. It's about catering a picnic. You say, I thought it might be good for explaining about holidays. They could talk about their own feast days and celebrations and maybe bring food the next week.

I ask if the sound quality's good, or if, at least, the movie's funny.

I don't know, you say. You offer to go to the AV room for the video. You offer to show me the newsletter you got in the mail about teaching ESL in Europe.

And so on, until we get to Devon, where you have to turn off to go home. After a few steps you turn around and wave, as if to say, No hard feelings, and I smile and walk a half block to the El, climb up to the platform, and settle onto a bench to wait. I look down in your direction, even though you're bound to be out of sight by now; I see only winking cars and the outline of trees that stand in front of the lake, strangers on the other side of the platform. I look down at my naked hands and know without having to tell myself: This is how my life will be from now on, forever.

# Living with Moranza

I am living with Moranza. He is doe-eyed as the Degas self-portrait sitting on the fireplace mantel. We live in the kind of house that complacent married couples own, though we aren't and we rent. It's on a tree-lined street, but all is not idyllic; we have to move our cars from one side of the street to the other every day. No parking odd-numbered days, no parking even-numbered days. We often have to park three streets away. Then we wander the way I do whenever I park in the three-tiered garage at O'Hare, except if you lose your car there, you can call on the emergency phone and someone will tell you where your car is. It's done by computer, proving this is a city with heart. Capitalism with a human face.

Moranza is working for the *Tribune*, writing the long, featurey kind of articles both of us used to write when we worked for the paper in Miami. I have turned from words to pictures. In art you are allowed to reach in and extract the images from your dreams. Moranza doesn't like my new intaglio series, *Dreaming Confessionals*, but still he says, You're terrific. I teach printmaking twice a week and he comes up to me as I grade projects at the dining room table (a beautiful thing, wooden and sleek, like some kind of near-extinct animal) and kisses the back of my neck. He says, Oh my lovely, my beautiful bubble-bath princess.

I have tried to train him not to say this, but the sound of it intrigues him too much. It no longer annoys me and I can respond, Your profile is lovely, even as I'm looking forward. I see it in my head. Have done it in charcoals, rubbing with the tips of my fingers to make his smudgepot eyes. Here, Degas, I say, my Cleopatra Valentino, I say, my Rudy Vallee, *mi Diego mi Rivera mi corazón*, and then one or both of us turn out the lights.

I used to do that in Miami all the time—make up nicknames for everyone, fitting and un-; slogans, alliterative and non-. For one office party I made fortune cookies, marked them so each person received, as I said then, his just dessert. I thought up the team song for the annual softball game, came up with the right few words for birthday cards, headlines faster than some of the editors. Moranza wasn't bad either but couldn't be bothered with those kinds of details.

But those things didn't really matter. On big stuff, he let out the stops. When he was good he was great. They hired him because he spoke Spanish, but he got along better than anyone else did with pureblood Wasps. He did his best piece on a football player, a giant man written in a giant's language. That worked. One about a wealthy but tragic widow—on Mother's Day—barely did. You had to keep him away from pathos and sunsets and the ocean or else he'd bleed purple so you couldn't see a thing through the haze of adjectives. Moranza's on a roll, Schwartzman would say. Schwartzman was the smartass rock critic who kept track of everyone's spurts, told us when we were doing well, said that a writer will outdo himself three months of the year, then the next person in the department will pick up steam, all unconsciously. Moranza's rolls lasted for five, six months at a time. The boy had rhythm.

Then he'd ingeniously combine his vacation and comp time and parlay them into junkets to Egypt and India and Indonesia. Spain, he said, Mexico—they're too easy.

There was a time Moranza was going to write a book. He set aside one night to unfold the idea before me. We were in the Italian restaurant on the Boulevard. A whole rowdy tableful of people from the city desk came in right after us. Thought we were very tête-à-tête but we weren't. We were talking about the plot, a spinoff of a feature he'd written about Key West and pirate treasure. He had been sent to interview that bounty hunter everyone ended up writing about—the *New York Times, Life, Time.* He deserved the assignment and I'd felt straight-out happy for him, no preceding stab of jealousy to smooth out inside. I admired his plot too, the way he could change reality through his imagination—again, no pain of envy. I told him so.

By then I hadn't been on a roll in so long it almost blew Schwartzman's theory. I was trying too hard but couldn't stop myself. I was reaching. I'd been at the paper seven years straight. I'd wanted politics, but they sent me to features and I'd stayed. I don't remember when I started feeling that every story had to be different, a statement about writing, a dazzler. I was a chef who wouldn't prepare the same meal twice, wasn't even content with variations. Everything had already been done. I was straining, a runner who kept searching for new strides, a diver who kept going farther and farther down, looking for some bright new sea creature. I began to analyze. Even as I wrote, I would classify the type of lead I was writing, suddenly recalling the category from my grad-school journalism texts. That's a house-of-cards construction, I'd think. The old anecdotal. The twister. Moranza and I worked on a story together about hurricanes and I admired the ingenuity of the weather service when it came to names. Computer banks full of them. I began to think I'd keep my own records. I spent half a Saturday in the office charting my topics and styles from the past year. I hid them in my computer directory, naming the file *Sense.*

That's when I decided that those who can't choose, choose to wander. I had wandered from art classes into journalism school, and I wandered out of the journalism world back into art. Started spending hours at night with the newspapers' illustrators, watching, copying, testing—wandered across the room from features to graphics. Just as years before Moranza had wandered into the features department. No, that's not right. He flew. Straight and sure as an arrow, into the desk beside me.

Moranza didn't stick with the book. He spent one day calling agents on the company WATS, then went on a trip to the Panhandle to gather preelection moods. He drank lots of beer and got lots of color. In the office he kept repeating a quote from a local judge: I was born at night, but I wasn't born last night. I admired the way he mixed in with the rednecks. The series was almost brilliant, just a touch condescending. It was really my kind of story. Or had been. After that I began to get tense when I had to talk to anyone who wasn't white collar. Before, I could breeze through anything. I was an actress always on. I could talk to anyone because I wasn't Ceci, the bubble-bath princess, I was Ceci, reporter, who could squeeze blood from a stone. Always got my quote. Got inside the houses of jurors who wouldn't talk to anyone else. Forced myself to make that second and third and tenth phone call. Always the right amount of banter to relax them. But take the notebook away, and I was just the princess again. Tongue-tied.

The time I won a national AP award, *People* magazine called me. Offered me a salary that I got the paper to match. Everyone would tell me, Try Washington, New York, even Philly's a step up, but I waited. Whenever I imagined moving up, I saw a building that got narrower at the top. To go up was to close off. I realized my perspective was from the ground.

But after Moranza's election story, I turned back into the bubble-bath princess. I reverted—porcelain was shining through the common clay. I was afraid I'd be found out—my folksiness a sham—would dream of discovery, the flash of Aha! in the middle of the night. I felt like traveling royalty, always having to hide my identifying strawberry birthmark. Not that I was a Rockefeller or anything—I was just the second daughter of the largest independent bubble-bath manufacturer in the country. All that meant was we traveled in Europe in the summers and were used to shopping at Neiman's every week with credit cards. And that grocery stores and dry cleaners delivered. And that we had a vacation house and knew the soft solid heft of good silver. And that in high school I'd felt separate from the normal flow of the world, as if I were looking down on it, like Rapunzel or Sleeping Beauty.

My father was the first to call my sister and me the bubble-bath princesses. The first time *Forbes* called him a mogul he asked me at breakfast all week, How is my Mogulette doing? Did the Mogulette sleep well last night? My sister, the other princess, was already away at college.

We would eat in the kitchen, at the expensively installed oak counter from the deli he ran before he went back to work for his father. This reminds me of my roots, he'd say, and he always carefully wiped the wood himself with a damp cloth, pounding it affectionately, like a football teammate. But his roots were really in the bubble-bath factory his father had started, and the deli had been one last stab at independence after the war. I had to make a living, he'd say. And they needed me. He'd been the one who'd created the dancing Dolly, the Barnston Bubble Girl, that flashed in neon on the top of the factory.

Moranza said what he really wanted to do was run an inn in New England somewhere and do the cooking and the greeting and write his novel. His parents were even behind it, but instead Moranza stayed in Miami and worked on a series about stock-fraud scandals.

He loved prison interviews, loved talking to people with axes to grind. Jilted lovers, ex-wives. Called them by their first names, drove out to remote locations with a woman on parole for manslaughter. He sat on his desk and we laughed. Watch out, Moranza, we said. Look what happened to the last guy she liked.

It was a night like this. It was a going-away party for someone I'd seen once at a staff meeting who was moving from one neighborhood bureau to another. Everyone was drunk and there was a constant series of pie-throwing incidents and jokes I didn't quite understand.
I decided to throw a pillow at the next person who walked in. It was Moranza. I barely knew him then. He'd just moved to my department from the Key West bureau. We walked out together at 5:00 A.M. when the party broke up. It was still dark enough to see stars and you could hear birds and bugs and cars down the main streets. When we walked to our cars he kissed me. We drove to his place on South Beach and looked across the bay at the newspaper building and went to sleep. In the morning, we walked to brunch at the Cordozo overlooking the ocean. He told me an involved story about drug smugglers on Sugarloaf Key. We could tell that the woman alone at the next table was listening. It's true, he told her. It was in the newspaper. It was in the paper because he wrote it. Then our eggs came, steaming, garnished with wafer-thin orange wedges and a little curl of kale, and the woman at the next table lost interest in our conversation.

We were always together. He'd be away from his desk and they'd say, Where's Moranza? I never knew but I always knew. How should I know? I'd say, then: He's in the john. And he'd come back from the john. Or: He went downstairs for coffee. And sure enough he'd come back, Styrofoam cup in hand. He would infuriate me when we'd go to lunch or coffee: on the way he'd stop at the john—to make a pit stop, as he'd say—and I'd be alone standing in the hallway. Nothing to do. Nothing to read. Alone waiting for Moranza.

He wasn't that special. Just a beautiful dark-eyed Mexican-American Degas with language that would lift you up like a carpet. He tried too hard, could write hard and gaudy, aluminum lawn ornaments shining in your eyes, glinting in the sun. Tried always for the classical allusion, tried to push it, to bend things to fit. Didn't always work but he tried. We all tried.

One Sunday I was in the little room where they kept the old Who's Whos and he kissed me. I never knew why. He already had his girlfriend then.

When I got to Chicago I went to a career counselor who fed me tea and sandwich cookies while some workmen repaired her driveway. I told her I was thinking about going back to ESL—despite all my other experience. She told me to write a book from an article I'd done on immigration law. She gave me someone's name and I called and found out he only published textbooks. I could have called around but it didn't make sense to write it from the Midwest.

When I got a full-time offer to teach ESL and composition, I called the counselor back. She said, Don't do it. You'll be buried in student papers. You'll go crazy. It will be a slow painful death.

She was wrong. I am living with Moranza. We are professors of cultural history. Every year we write a book together. To be perfectly fair, we alternate the placement of our names. We are reviewed in the scholarly and popular journals. We are both far along on the tenure track.

She was wrong. I am living with Moranza. He is a consultant and still talks about writing his book. I am nearly famous as an artist. We live in a 1920s Prairie-style bungalow which is big enough and well made enough to muffle my hammering on Diet Dr Pepper cans. When they're flattened I wrap them around small ungainly parts of old cars I pick up in junkyards. I scrub myself with Lava every night, using up much hot water.

I am living with Moranza. We are architects. We have changed the shape of everything and are incredibly articulate. There are no cost overruns. Every columnist in Chicago has our unlisted number. They call frequently.

I am living with Moranza. He is a lawyer with a briefcase of new leather. I waterproof it and rub it with Meltonian shoe wax, a hint I read in "Dear Dorsey." He takes the commuter train home and brings me bouquets of newspapers. Pick one, he says, any one.

I am living with Moranza. He is a state senator. He is a frequent flyer to Springfield. He has his own campaign manager; he doesn't expect me to subvert my life for his. My pottery is at the Museum of Contemporary Art—on display and in the gift store. I worry about making dishes that are too delicate to be used. Perhaps this is just a continuation of the family legacy; except bubble bath, ephemeral as it is, has its practical side. It gets you clean and doesn't (at least Barnston's) leave a bathtub ring.

The art critics don't mention this lack of utility; this is the vogue. I write apologias for the fragility of art. They accompany my bio at each show.

I am living with Moranza. He gives away money for the foundation of a large corporation. We are always invited to fiestas and New Year's celebrations sponsored by community groups. I have learned Chinese, the language of the future. When I speak with his Asian beneficiaries, I am fluid and intimate.

I am living with Moranza. He is a snake hunter. In the summer we go to South America for two months. Deftly I interview corrupt politicians. He collects skins and venom. Together we have invented a sure cure for snakebite. We patent it.

I am living with Moranza. We are gypsy fortunetellers. We are 100 percent accurate.

I am living for Moranza. . . .

I host a public-radio show. I write scathing reviews. I am a director.
I am an actor. I have my own ballet company. I perform in a gallery. I
perform onstage. I perform on the subway. At Samuel's deli on Broad-
way there is a sandwich named for me.

My father used to take us to Fred's Texas Eatery, the successor to the
deli he sold before I was born. Right after we'd order, there would be an
awkward moment, when my dad would tell Fred that if he'd known
Fred would make a go of it, he'd have sold the place for double. Then
they'd both laugh and that would ease the way for Fred to talk about
his property tax bills, to shatter any assumption that we were entitled
to free hot dogs after all those years. At the same time, the banter
covered up my father's envy of Fred and his shame for his pride in the
factory you can see from the Eatery's front windows. Their joking
covered the uncertainty about what exactly had been my father's part
in the success of the family bubble-bath business. When it's team-
work, you don't know which partner should take credit, he'd say.

And I'd wait for my mother to say something like, Your father's just
being modest, everyone knows he's the marketing genius. But she
never did. She'd say, Selling the deli was the best decision you could
make at the time. Like a reporter who plays it right down the middle.
And I'd always think she would have been happier if he'd kept the
deli, though she used to tell me about those early days where he'd
work all morning and night and even Saturdays when, if we'd been
invited to a bar mitzvah, she'd go to services without him.

But I couldn't imagine how it had been much different from the
Saturday mornings I remembered, going to the synagogue with the
nervous family all worried about business, how he and my uncle
would look so distracted during the reception afterward, watching the
clock across the room even though they were wearing watches. Then
they'd drop us off downtown at Neiman's or Sakowitz while they
stopped in to see how things were at Barnston's Bubblers.

I think how my life might have been different if he'd kept the deli,
how I might have been able naturally, without advance preparation, to

walk into bars and church suppers and talk to people who didn't know what it was like to have a father who knew maître d's all across Europe and those gnomes of Zurich.

I wouldn't be royalty. I wouldn't be any princess.

In Miami, the editors watched me change and strain and flounder. They said, You need more training if you want to do graphics. Better stick with words. We'll move you to where style isn't that important. You'll just go out and report. Clean mean black and white. Simple.

And I did it for three months. Like a factory worker. Like a machine. But princesses aren't good in factories. They aren't good at grinding out the anonymous chuck that 90 percent of the world is interested in. The princess tried. But Anastasia never forgets the feel of real silk. The princess wishes she didn't feel the pea—she'd love to be able to sleep anywhere.

The day I thought, Anyone could do this, I took a long lunch and wrote a letter of resignation. Schwartzman saw it and said, Best thing you've written in months.

I am in the bathtub now, smelling the old familiar vanilla-nutmeg of Barnston's Bubblers original formula, molecules colliding throughout the room, accompanied by that special crunch of the foam. Moranza appears beside me. Do you want a back scrub? he asks. No, the bubble-bath princess murmurs. Do you want a nape massage? No, she murmurs, shuddering, shivering from the cold touch on her spine. Then he lights the white vanilla-nutmeg-scented candle that comes free with three box tops of Barnston's (romantic baths, the brainstorm of true marketing genius, has expanded Barnston's market share of the eighteen-to-thirty-five crowd), and he strips silently as a cat and without making a splash or sound, miraculously, as always, without displacing the water, Moranza steps into the tub behind me.

## The Crab

Situation: Your mother has cancer. The crab has taken her. Your boyfriend is at war. Or with war. He is in a broken little country, covering it, as they say. A little war. He is also at war with his mother. You have never met her. It would be a sign I didn't like you, he said, if I were to take you to meet her. Last Thanksgiving he went home, alone. You ate with some vegetarians. Two of them were Armenians with beautiful hair, teeth, and names—all those *k*'s and *h*'s. They knew people who had died in earthquakes on both sides of the world. And had forebears in the great massacre.

His mother keeps everything: twist-ems, plastic bags (washes them, like your vegetarian friends do), plastic bread-bag fasteners (as your mother does, storing them in a Sucrets tin). It's a sickness, your boyfriend says. At home he doesn't have a drawer full of twist-ems. He keeps a large jar of pennies, though, which you hide. He needs twist-ems, does without, ties the ends of plastic bags, a double knot, that you don't have the patience to open. But you do, cursing him. You don't tear them because you love him. Because you love him you don't tear them.

He is really your ex-boyfriend. He has torn your heart from you. Once he loved you, whole cloth. Whole body. Cunt, ass, hair too wild for him (too wild for your mother; probably, too, for his mother). He has torn himself from you, from your life, though he hasn't changed the code on his answering machine. You could check the messages, but no one called him when you were with him, when you loved him: no one but you, his mother, his troubled sister. (All the women in his life, named Trouble.) He reminded you of your mother. He was orderly. Crumbs sucked up in his Dustbuster. What he calls disorder you call normal. You write messages in dusty dresser tops, the way people write on cars and vans: Clean me. Clean me.

Your mother cleaned you. Your mother did everything, everything but give you the milk from her body. Before you were born she nourished you, as the body does when it is just body, doing what the body does and no more (directed or not directed by the mind). It was not scientific to give the milk from her body, your mother was no cow or pump or Mother Earth nourisher. The doctor, the expert, said it is no longer done and they gave her pills to dry up the milk.

Don't cry over unspilt.

Your large, round mother seems fragile, is teary-eyed. Shaky. Has told nobody about having this operation except the immediate family and her best friend. She will tell her second-best friend—only because otherwise the friend will be hurt. It would be hard to be in hiding from the world for five weeks flat on her back, her organs removed, the ones that fed you month after month, removed. Imagine a pear, say the books. In the book you buy her: one page of sketches, partial hysterectomy, total hysterectomy.

Hysterical female. Lunatic. Fringe.

She always tried to comb your hair. Brush it. Teased: I will come in the middle of the night and cut.

He would pretend to be stroking your head, then you would realize he was raking it with his fingers. Ever so subtly working out the curl. Mom! you would whine. The first boyfriend who reminded you of your mother.

On the phone you told your mother, I'll come a day early and we'll do creative visualizations. But you said it the wrong way. Like: You know it's good for you but you won't do it. The way she'd say: I'll come a day early and get you a haircut and a manicure. I've tried, she said. Stumbling. In my own way. All we can do is hope and hope. All we can do is hope and pray.

You wonder what her prayers are like. Each night, in the dark, she and your father said the Shema. Once only a few years ago you shared a hotel room with them and heard them. Like schoolchildren laying themselves down. In trust.

He would lay you down and you would lay him down and sometimes, rapture.

Licking breasts. His nipples, yours. The nights you could do nothing, for whatever reason—fears rising through your throat. He would stroke your hair. The one time he turned away, not now not now, you were crushed, could not understand how he had withstood your curved-away back, so many nights.

You talked while making love—laughed, tickled, rammed belly against hip, rassling. Pretended you had just met. Now yes oh darling—the things you would say.

He liked children. Bounced S's children on his knee as if he knew them. They called him the Man. They would ask you, How is the Man?

He is south now, where children are dying. He was a foreign correspondent in Thailand. He went to Vietnam—for press conferences. After the war. Wrote about Cambodia/Kampuchea/Khmer. At parties he was annoyed with people who only knew about the Jewish Holocaust. Oh, Cambodia, really? they would say. Elie Wiesel, you would tell him, talks about the genocide in Cambodia. When you'd say that, he'd never register a response. You don't know why.

Hysterectomy. Scrape out the woman in her. Womb.

You went to a seaside bed-and-breakfast place one weekend, alone, to rest after a winter of sickness. You'd had the flu on top of bronchitis. Every guest wrote comments in a book. You wrote: This has been the most nourishing place I've been since the womb. You meant it. Meant to shock too.

He ironed your clothes. Only once or twice. When you two were on vacation, he repacked your suitcase when you were out. To prove a point: that packing neat meant you could get more in. Which, you said, only made the suitcase heavier. Before the vacation, he bought you colored pens, a tiny flashlight, dry-roasted peanuts, little boxes of Cheese Nips, an inflatable pillow, bright new socks. You were like his child. Receiving so much.

The day you left his house his iron fell from the ironing board. Even though it was carpet, it broke. He said this. Ruefully. Too sad to be amused. A fitting end.

He appreciates you, seems to, your mother said when she met him, seems like a nice young man. Twenty, thirty times a day you imagine him holding your face, appreciating.

When you told S that he ironed your clothes, even the complicated pants, she said: Marry him. After all, he liked her children, all children.

He wanted you to be a mother. How could you be a mother? He was your mother.

Would you have wanted me if I'd wanted children? you asked him. He sat you on the couch, like telling an employee that the gig is up, whatever a gig is. Or was it jig? Did he feel the thrill of control, of power, of, Now I'm sitting her down on my couch to tell her the gig or jig is up? I am like a water buffalo, he'd said at the beginning, an image he'd picked up in Thailand, I will take so much without complaint and then one day I'll explode. He sounded disappointed that you two had never yelled. As if that meant something was missing. Something that would make it a clean break.

So now he is in the middle of a little war, watching. Asking questions: Are you dead or alive? What is death like? What does it wear? Are its teeth dull or pointed? Have you looted a store today? How do you and your neighbors get reinforcements for your ammunition?

When he returns and finally calls, you will argue about politics. He as always will be world-weary. He will say, We had to go down there, but it was not as necessary as the military would have us believe.

Your mother's operation is over. Everything looks fine, says the doctor, all the cancer gone. Though further tests are pending. Tests are pending and your mother looks like death, like waxen death, you could touch her hair, her face, the skin of her face is slack. She looks like she had a face-lift, the skin drooping over the sides, over the edges, so that her skin is smooth. Though it droops like curtains on her neck. The nurses yell at her: Hello hello take a deep breath cough. She raises her eyebrows. Her eyes swollen shut, crusted together. You tell your mother they put makeup on her, a wan joke—it looks like mascara but it is some kind of Vaseline. Her face is octagonal shaped like in the pictures of her as a child. Touch her skin and get no reaction. This is how it will be when she's dead. It will be like this, here but not here. Yelling at her to come back. Last night they brought in something else to sign, new disclaimers on the doctor's forms. All the parts of her body that could be removed. All the things that could go wrong. She shivered, she cried a little. Surprised: They didn't tell me about this. Appendix, bladder, intestine, breasts, everything that they could take. She shivered in grief, powerless over the contingencies. Coma, death. She read it all, she signed her name. You sat there, able to do nothing but rub her back.

Like this. Like this.

## The Children Who Swim from You

Ruben and Ruthie met at a party when she was in her young twenties. He was nearly ten years older. Neither drank; rather, they stood next to the cheese-and-crackers tray, almost close enough to feel the other's breaths, talking above the music. Ruthie was large and wide and she stooped to appear smaller and thinner. She had smooth wavy hair the color of burnt sienna—a most perfect color, she thought when she allowed herself the sin of vanity. Ruben had light curly hair and a neck like a chicken's. His hands were strong, strangely muscular. He had grown up working. Ruthie had grown up mainly inactive, among hard workers. She knew about injustice but didn't know how to fight it. Ruben had been in the world war, the one that came after the war to end all wars. He helped to end it.

Ruben was in business for himself. He had broken away from the family bubble-bath business and had figured out how to get a lease and make contracts with restaurant and food supply companies so that he had what he needed to run his delicatessen. He never ran out of napkins or toothpicks. The cupboard was never bare.

Ruthie had always wanted a man who was active in the world, making deals and signing documents handed to him by strangers. She liked the idea of a man who worked in a place with strong smells—pickles, onions, salami. She also found him handsome. Ruben thought Ruthie was beautiful, round like a cherub. She thought of herself as a pudgy brown-haired person with a handsome older brother and beautiful younger sister. The brother was confident. The sister was indulged and grew pleasant on indulgence. Ruthie was big and felt awkward and she worried.

Ruben really was tall, medium tall for a man. He spoke well in public and in private and he could imitate accents—Brooklyn, Eastern European, Deep South. His animation pleased Ruthie.

She had one bathing suit. It was black (slenderizing), stretched, as she said to herself with horror and also humor, to the gills. She had grown up during the 1930s polio scare and was afraid to swim, so sat softly dipping her toes in and out of the community pool. While her sister swam laps, Ruthie would sit on the edge of the pool and wonder about what her life would be if she were someone else.

Ruben worked hard. He made business decisions every day as they came up. He was not a scholar. He had some theories, but they all explained practicalities. He did not wonder how many devils or angels could dance on the head of a pin or prance through the eye of a needle. He himself did not like to dance. But he had a primitive belief in God. He believed in a divine plan and in divine order. He believed he did not have the wherewithal to discern celestial cause and effect. But he trusted deeply, so implicitly that if he'd had doubts, he wouldn't have been able to put them into words.

Ruben and Ruthie were married six months after meeting. Their luggage was stolen on their honeymoon in New York City. They came back to a new brick ranch house in Houston with flowerbeds.

Ruben and Ruthie had trouble procreating. She took her temperature. He was awkward discussing such things. It had felt foreign to hear the other soldiers during the war talk about sex, to laugh about episodes with prostitutes. He could not convince himself they were not making it up. For her it was a duty; this is what you did when you married. Her cousin had given her a book, which she hid in the drawer where she kept her sanitary napkins in their pale blue box. The book talked about pleasure and graceful-sounding positions. She was not good at either. She was better at pain and awkwardness. Ruben and Ruthie coupled like well-meaning fish in the wrong kind of tank. There were many excuse-me's. Sometimes they forgot themselves. She whispered under her breath: He loves me he loves me.

She gave birth twice, under anesthesia.

She loved the babies. Equally. That's what she told them.

Ruben loved them; he called them his strange little seals. He made things to amuse them—kites, comic books with their names on them, balsa-wood figures of ducks—and sometimes held them.

*Ruthie would hold one seal on her lap and put her juicy lips under the flippers and putputputter like a lawn mower. (She did have her playful side.) She would pretend she was eating chocolate candies. Ooo there's a good one, she would say. Ooo there's a coconut raspberry cream. Ptui! and she'd pretend to spit it out on the floor. The little seals clamored and yelped.*

*Or she would lay them in bed and cover them with the sheet and bedspread and sit down hard next to them and say, What are these lumps? Is this a rock? Oh it must be a pillow.*

*The little seals did not mind Ruthie at all.*

*But Ruthie minded the seals. They were slippery and full of sleek fine hair that they shed all over her carpet. And the mess in the bathtub! They could not clean it up very well themselves because instead of hands they had flippers.*

*The seals grew up and at nineteen each transformed into a mermaid, breasts open to the wind.*

*When they came to visit, they would sit patiently as Ruthie arranged seaweed artfully to hide their delicate parts.*

*The mermaids would dash water on Ruben and Ruthie. Ruben and Ruthie would shiver. The mermaids would try to dance. They wished they'd been taught how. They wished it didn't hurt quite so much.*

## The Window of Vulnerability

Stephen's house is shaded by trees. Covered by trees. You can't tell what it looks like, only that it's wooden, two stories, the kind of house a single man wouldn't live in alone.

His father lived with him. Died there. Died in the hospital but he died in the house—his clothes, his paintbrushes there. Who is there to tell you how to clean out a house? To clean out death from your house the precise way you search out *hametz*, unleavened foods, on Passover, chasing the crumbs symbolically with a feather and wooden spoon? No feather large enough to lift the contents of his father's closets.

Upstairs, rooms like a flea market. Like the warehouse of a gallery. Canvases stacked. Clippings stacked. Nothing inventoried. You cannot inventory an artist's life if he is your father.

And downstairs, there are books and dust in every room. In the living room, stacks of *Commentary.* Travel guides to Israel in the bathrooms. Years of *Time* and *National Review* in the kitchen. Slivers of mold float in coffee cups on windowsills. Empty brown grocery bags stand side by side in the kitchen. Tall giant empty Coke bottles are lined up next to them, not rinsed out.

There are no bugs. There are advantages to living in a cold climate.

In Stephen's office at the university is a green blackboard filled with lists. Books on foreign policy stacked haphazardly on shelves. Pencil shavings on the floor.

Every school morning he eats at the Place, the diner written up in a national guidebook for being both quaint and au courant. He and his father would walk there every morning for eggs. He orders alone now: two eggs, hard scrambled, with ketchup on the side. Sometimes, at night, for a snack, he returns. He is from Pittsburgh, home of the Heinz Co. Whenever he has ketchup or mustard, he thinks of that.

The diner hires fat old women who look like they have always worked there and Cleopatra-eyed punks with spiky hair who either deal drugs or create art. The Place is near north campus, by the art school. Usually Stephen talks to Mike the busboy, who sometimes sells acid at the head shop in the downtown mall. Each of them appreciates the other's humor. It makes each proud to trade jokes with his political enemy. Stephen is planning to vote for Reagan.

One night Stephen is waited on by Ceci, an art student who wears a stegosaurus hairdo of five wedges on her scalp. For some reason she hands him the morning *Register*, and looking at the headlines he read twelve hours ago gives him a pang he thought he had outgrown. He sees her black-nailed hand, her long white fingers, and he thinks of the way his father would give him the paper with a little cough, and years before that, the way he himself would collect the rolled paper from the front yard as if it were a gift, as if it were manna, and would snap the string and present it, smoothed flat, to his wife while she got out the butter to soften. And he thinks of hands that touch and clasp and wear promises but never change their shapes to hold those promises, and he knows: It will be impossible to go home alone tonight.

It is just after Ceci's shift. She and Stephen make new tracks in new snow. It is quiet, the way of small towns after midnight, the traffic lights flashing yellow. They hear cars hissing at the bottom of the hill. Stephen is wearing the red sneakers and faded jeans he always wears. Gray hairs are overtaking his dark bushy beard and hair so it looks like they too are fading.

In his living room he feeds her Ak-Mak crackers and green Chinese tea. He shows her what a Taiwanese student showed him, how to find the paths of *chi*, energy, in the body. He stands bent over in his shabby living room, still wearing his thin coat with flimsy fringes of wolf hair around the hood, and stays like this until his legs begin to vibrate.

He is triumphant.

Then the *chi* goes up, out through the head, he says.

She wants to be an artist who works for world peace. She is open to *chi*, up to a point, but does not have time in her life now to develop a deep understanding. She wants to learn welding first. She wants to learn how to make paper out of lumpy objects, and how to perform civil disobedience.

I know what everyone thinks of me, he says. He knows that every-one at school and in town makes fun of him. He's the right-winger who looks like a Red. Who dresses like a Red, who drives a jalopy like one.

Who utterly fears the Russians.

She shrugs.

It is hard, in a small liberal college town with a small liberal col-lege, to find others who fear the Soviet Union. Especially if you always wear your frayed jeans and red sneakers everywhere, even to cocktail parties for distinguished visiting professors.

She wants to make him laugh. She doesn't want to believe what he believes. She donates small sculptures to sell at the local Peace Fair every summer and she signs nuclear-freeze petitions. She sends letters to her congresspeople. It is her own government that she distrusts. She does not want to hear that she should worry about the Soviet government and SS-20s and the fate of Western Europe.

Much less Eastern.

She does not feel threatened by the window of vulnerability.

He is known for sitting in the back of the auditorium when the supporters of détente are speaking and to ask three-minute questions that are really challenges. Once a former senator, a Democrat, tried to hit him. The act aroused much sympathy in the public until the next lecture.

He is in the mathematics and statistics department. Once he had a fellowship in Italy and much promise. He is an associate professor. He is not rising. He has sidled over into economics and devises courses comparing Eastern and Western market systems. He publishes in small conservative journals of international affairs. He has tenure.

He shows Ceci his father's paintings. He was a genius, he says. Snow falls hard against the windows. Stephen thinks of the bird, won-ders if he should tell her about the bird. A year ago, or two, a bird flew into his bedroom, the room he'd shared with the wife who left, left him with a baby carriage they thought they'd need someday.

He could hear it from downstairs, knocking about. He ran upstairs. The bird had flown straight into the bedroom. It was black. Or else it was white, the room dark, and he could see flashes of the white whirring thing. Was it frightened?

He doesn't tell her about this. He gives her the chronology of his father's talent, how he would paint every night after dinner, except Saturdays. He tells her about the time his father's studio burned a week before his first and only show in New York City. The whole building was destroyed and his father took down all his pictures in the house and sold every one of them. After that, he devoted himself to his dental practice and only painted on weekends.

Stephen tells her of Pittsburgh, the fountain at the Point, where the three rivers meet. He tells her about the little place you can order hot dogs and a barrel of fries all day and all night, and how you can walk from there down the street to Pitt and its Cathedral of Learning with its soot-covered walls.

He was a smart boy, everyone said. Would go far. Become famous. He loved math. Well, didn't particularly love it, but could do it. Loved to get lost in it. Had to work hard to enter that labyrinth. Didn't want to leave it once he found his way in.

He never learned how to dance but has taken to these Chinese exercises like a duck to water. Amazing, really.

Ceci pours more tea. The father's paintings, she thinks, are dark. Can't see much in them. Sometimes, though, she doesn't react to art until months later, and bam, there's the image. Socks her in the middle of serving a plate of eggs and hash browns.

That's why she works at the diner. Gives her time to think, to sort out the images.

He was always quiet at the Place, spending a half hour on one page of the *Register.* She doesn't know why she offered him the paper tonight. Just to see if he'd notice he'd seen it before? Just to see if he actually did read the paper when he sat there staring at it in the morning?

He reminds her of the curator at the county historical society museum—a collector who gathers and names but never steps back to see what he has. She wonders if he can even speak about what he has read. There is something undigested about him, about the opinions he drones from the back of assembly halls. She wonders if she could describe the historical museum to him, without telling him what brought it to mind. She wonders and can see its piles of things: shelves of ladies' gloves, baskets of antique calling cards. The old curator would conduct a tour, saying, Here are the hats, here are the gloves, these are the fans the ladies used to flirt behind. Here is a room of medical equipment.

Ten black doctors' bags on the floor.

That image comes back to her often, unexpectedly. The first time was early one morning when she was bringing oatmeal to two construction workers. Those doctors' bags just lying there, no one ever going to use them again.

She could see Stephen carrying a dusty old bag like that.

Her hair reminds him of birds.

It was weather like this, new snow, when it flew into the bedroom. Stephen followed the sounds upstairs, trailing gray trickles of slush. He turned on the light in the room, the site of many cries and flutters as he had tried to lose himself in another labyrinth, as he had tried to maneuver a merging of selves.

This is when he kisses her. The top part of each triangle in her hair is hardened with gel. Underneath and in between each wedge, it is soft. Smells like old roses. His face is the most comfortable she's ever touched with her face. Cuddly like a family pet.

He felt the whisper of the flush of feathers. He hadn't wanted to catch it. He'd wanted it to land on his shoulder. Stephen, tamer of wild things, the man who harnesses equations. Who understands balance of power on a global scale.

The role of the artist, Ceci is thinking, is to find the universality of humankind. To bind unlike peoples. To destroy differences. Be ambassador to souls.

The bird was black. He was sure of it. It banged into the walls. He could hear the smash. He opened the window. He struggled with the storm window. He laid the screen on the floor.

Wild things need to be in the wild. The yin and the yang of nature. A tree by the window dripped snow. Big soggy puffs of it.

That was the only time he'd felt like painting, like grabbing a brush right then and describing what he'd seen. What he'd experienced. To be an artist, he thought, and feel this all the time, this urgency. He missed his father then. Thought, What would he do? Could he have painted something he'd seen so briefly?

Would it then become his father's bird?

Ceci is thinking of wings. She is thinking of flight. She is thinking of energy flowing through her, up through her toes to the peaks of her mini-mohawks. Close your eyes, she says out loud. Close them. Look at nothing. She covers his eyes with her hand.

Stephen and Ceci are lying on a blue vinyl couch marked with coffee rings. He wonders how women always seem to know which product will remove stains. He wonders if the bird made a mess that he never found, if the first time he brings a woman upstairs, she'll see it. Blank blank blank, she whispers. He starts to repeat it. Says Blank. Blank.

He opens his eyes. Can't help it. Opens them, stares straight into the blue-and-red acrylic painting, *Abraham Sacrificing Isaac.* By his father. Completed many, many years ago.

# The Average Man

The man says, I'm average-looking. He says, That's how you'll know me, I'm average-looking. He doesn't say, I'm about average when it comes to good-looking. What he says he says almost with pride, not quite. Ceci has heard his voice three times. Recorded, all three times. You can tell a lot from a man's voice, a whole lot from his answering machine's outgoing message. She's hung up on several, dozens. Hey there, some of them say. Or there's blaring music. Or TV and film voices. Boris Badenov, Bullwinkle J. Moose, Bart Simpson, Brando—all the same, derivative. Sign of an unoriginal mind. She also hates motorcycle engine sounds. Or when they say: You know what to do. It's not the words, it's the tone. The smarminess. This man's voice is even, even keel. Average. The mythical average man. Which doesn't mean normal. By a long shot. Would the normal man—well, isn't it just an extension of power relations in the real world? Wherever that is.

The normal man, the average man, is waiting for her, in the lobby of a restaurant on Michigan Avenue. He's wearing a suit. It's an average suit, maybe an above-average suit. He'd suggested a snack. She felt he'd wanted lunch. She'd said coffee to his answering machine. He said coffee to hers, maybe a roll. The way he said *roll*, he sounded like a father talking about a quick Sunday breakfast, early morning, a man from her father's generation, not a man who looks up personal ads in the back of *City Life*, under the heading Special Needs/Desires. That would be a man who knew scones. Ruggelah, turtle cheesecake, the fare of coffeehouses. A cappuccino man, an espresso man, someone who'd been to Europe. Or at least Wicker Park. Not just places like this, where tourists might go to rest between shops or businessmen might stop in for a tête-à-tête.

A waiter seats them. Just coffee, she tells the waiter. The man's name is Al. That's what he tells her. Ceci has said her name is Cathy.

A dumb name, but that's one of the ones she uses. She used to tell them exotic lush names, but they'd say things like: Veronica, that suits you, a twinkle in the eye, perhaps, because he knew as well as she did that that wasn't anywhere near her name.

The average man looks around fifty-five, has brown hair, flecks of gray. Tanned wrinkled forehead, aviator glasses. At this late date. He looks like a banker. A loan officer. She doesn't want to know. She does. She wants to know what he does all day, what runs through his fingers. He's fingering the menu. He looks it up and down, as if comparing prices, as if calculating how much each item would weigh or speculating about the number of calories. She holds her breath, irritation in her solar plexus. She'd said coffee. He'd said coffee, a roll. Not lunch. It's 2:15. A Coke. She should have said a Coke. Give me a fucking break, Ceci says silently. You promised. I don't have time. Or I do have time but we didn't agree to lunch, a meal. This is just get-acquainted. That's what we said on the phone. Between appointments, he said, I'll have time to meet you, to go over particulars, if you'd like. To make sure this would work, we're talking the same—ah—language. Between appointments for him, between chores for her. Kinko's, the library, a newsstand to get a neighborhood paper for the ESL class she's teaching tonight. She needs time to prepare for the lesson: filling out job applications. She'll pair the students up: job interviewer, job interviewee. Pairs and one group of three, if there's an odd number of students.

Her eyes sidle around. Is he looking at the list of sandwiches? His eye on the first menu panel. He looks fierce. His eyes are fierce. Is his mouth? Is it set? Is his jaw clenched? If he was to unclench it she'd be able to tell if it was clenched in the first place. No sandwich, only dessert, she telegraphs. How dare he—you can get up now, Ceci, she tells herself. Leave.

But the flush is spreading, from there, she's wet, dammit, and flushes up to her stomach, up to her forehead, and again, stronger. Maybe this is it, she thinks. He's starting early on. At the beginning. Before the beginning, before we agree overtly. Maybe she's already said yes to the unmoving wrinkle lines, the flexing hands, the dark hairs between his knuckles, the hairs that rise ever so slightly in the draft from the opening door.

And he's just waiting for me, she thinks, waiting for me to object, to give him a chance to pull me out of there, and take me, and we'll go—where?

What will he do to me?

# The Last Day of the World

On the last day of the world, I would pass by those striding models at Neiman's whose black mink coats sit on them like dark refrigerators, and if they tried to hand me flyers about winter fur sales, I would hiss and sneer, No thanks, no thanks, I'm not going to see another winter, and you won't either, tootsie.

On the last day of the world I would ignore all my doctors' instructions which are taped on the real refrigerator at home.

I would not turn to God either.

I would cancel all doctor's appointments, with or without forty-eight hours' notice.

I would throw away my guide to food rotation for better health. I would not do my yoga. I would not imagine my healthy cells chomping on the cancer cells like rabbits or beavers or huge tough lions. I would not imagine anything. I would look. Stare at the world. Drink it.

I would eat slice after slice of pure-butter pound cake, and a Caesar salad, bowls of chopped liver, don't spare the schmaltz. More, more, clapping my hands as if calling for dancing girls. Snap snap, garçon, a lively look to ya. I would rap loudly on the empty bowl. I would order everyone around. I would not say *please* and *thank you.* I would not tip.

I would go to the ice-skating rink at the Galleria despite my weak ankles but I would refuse to put on skates. I would slide around, playing tag with strangers. Playing statues. After being touched, I would slowly slowly come back to life, joint by joint, like a flower blossoming in a Disney movie.

I would litter, smoke, spit, and play a radio in defiance of all posted and announced regulations.

I would ignore God's rules. I would not recite the Shema or light candles or blow the ram's horn on the mantel. I would not say Kaddish.

I would dismiss the émigrée who drives me around. I would grab the keys from her and drive to Chicago to see Ceci. I would ask her: Do I talk too much, really, really, do I? And when you said you tuned out 5 percent, was that an average, and if so, what was the highest percentage during any one day or conversation?

I would call Ellen at her office and sing "O Sole Mio" over and over. I would say, That's what you get for taking your mom to a movie with a cheap Italian soundtrack. I would appear behind her desk as she talked to the assistant-assistant, my hands over her eyes, Guess who, I'm sure you're dying to find out. There is no emergency to tend to. I would push up the ends of her lips to make a smile.

I would drive into dangerous zones, the Third Ward. I would leave my car and wait for buses alongside bundled-up old ladies. I would ask after their families, their feet. I would say I know, I know, when they talked of gout, varicosa. I would feel my thick blood pushing through the arteries to the end of my limbs, warming my feet.

I would meet a young Palestinian in front of city hall and bed him among the flowers, making sure he moved slowly slowly down my side. My touch would be gentle as satin. He would be my baby bird. We would coo. He would be my English muffin, my bright young biscuit, my hot red soup. Our great thirsts would be boundless, almost sated. Nothing in our way: no pain, no discomfort, nothing missing or sore. We would finish in time for a slow long walk before sundown. Strolling, he would tell me what it was like to live without a home. His anger would cause him to leap. I would follow until we were skipping through the zoo laughing and linking arms in some complicated but spontaneous way. We would push into a crowd outside the monkey house, shouting, We're special, we're special, move down.

We would stroll down the paths along the bayou, urging the joggers and power-walkers to slow down. I would yell, Notice the Spanish moss that hangs from the trees like wise men's beards, look into the shine of the grackles' feathers, that shine is like the rainbow you can see in spilled oil. I would importune couples holding hands: Kiss dammit kiss. I am your godmother.

I would play in the mud wherever I found it. I would cut down honeysuckle vines (both pink and white flowers) whenever I found them and wrap them around my head and arms and ankles. Bending easily.

I would follow anyone who said, Look at this.

I would find a garden to lie in and smell the earth, among tender shoots of lilies. I would call to the Palestinian: One more time, among all this green and moist black.

I would not worry about the at-home help stealing from me or the collapse of the market or intermarriage among our young people. I would understand the thrill of the exotic.

I would find a fabric store and at the demonstration table whip up some gold harem pants and parade in them until everyone looked into my face and said, All this, and she sews her own clothes, too.

I would interrupt anyone talking about the mind and body in a lofty distant way, with that gloss of I-know-it-all in his voice. I would write Ruben a note. Crowded by desperation, I would know what to say. I don't blame you for your decline. I see now that our bodies are innocent. I tried to learn love from the never-ending months of your illness.

I would burn the note in a public blaze, watch the smoke follow the wind, and I would leave before the fire trucks came.

I would address an envelope to the Palestinian—no card, only leaves from the garden. Knobby acorns, firm rosehips. I would save a rosehip for myself, fasten it to my blouse.

I would not take my medicine at all.

I would climb (for once, easily, so easily: scamper, as if light, as if nothing but bones and wire) to the rooftop of the Galleria and ask God why—not so much why now, but why all this pain up till now. And the quiet, the dreadful quiet. I would tell him I'm glad for that trip to his country, Israel. I would not cry. I would watch the firemen tending to the blaze. I would not pray for rain.

Would I arrange a protest? Would I desecrate some holy shrine?

Among the clouds, God would appear, his voice not familiar and not strange, telling me that he is the one who would cry, all alone, at the end. Because I refused to rage; he would mourn because I did not beg for terms, like Abraham seeking to waylay destruction. I would think (and he would read my thoughts): The end of the world is too tempting. The temptation is the escape from all consequences.

Abraham did not believe in escaping consequences.

I should bargain. I should bargain for my people, but I have no people. I cry up to God: I will not bargain with a terrorist. I give you back your angel of death in its original casing. Why is it up to me?

There is and is not this God. Let us say there is not this God. There is only the end of the world. And on the last day of the world I eat the world until there is no world. I kiss the stranger deeply, a gulp. We drink each other. I take the rosehip to my mouth, my nose, inhaling deeply. I sniff the garden dirt in the creases of my palms. On the last day of the world I would lift platefuls of liver, of *grebenes*, gefilte fish with *chrain*, slices of brisket, lox piled high and higher on bagels, offerings, raise my eyes to the horizon, not hungry, waiting.

# Sheets

A Jew who dies is supposed to be clothed in a simple sheath. Simple sheet. Winding sheet. Everyone is equal in death. Everyone is equal at birth, clothed in blood and other less palatable but no less universal substances. When I was young I followed "The Heart of Juliet Jones" in the funny papers and when Juliet bought a sheath I asked my mother what it was. A plain dress without a belt, my mother said. It was the sixties, just before the advent of the paper dress.

A *shomer*, a watcher, is supposed to sit with the dead and recite psalms. You can hire someone to do that, someone from, say, the *chevra kadisha*, the burial society. The funeral home takes care of it. The funeral home we use is a light brick building behind a crape myrtle tree with small flowers that look torn. The funeral home is familiar by now. The men and women who work there wear suits. They don't smile when I ask about volume discounts. Ellen and I are not the first pair of newly made orphans, losing two parents in two years, that they have seen. The world is full of orphans, after all, orphans much younger than my sister and me.

We have a choice; we can choose a plain coffin or a less plain one with a Jewish star carved on it, still plain enough to qualify for the approval of the Orthodox. One reason to like the Orthodox after all— they believe in plain pine boxes. Or oak. Or mahogany. They don't believe in satin and velvet lining and ornate carvings. They believe in wood and sheaths. And the Orthodox provide a chorus of volunteers (men for males, women for females) who wash and clean the dead. It is a holy task. I have no idea who makes up the *chevra* in Houston. Perhaps they're *lamed-vovniks*, the legendary thirty-six people whose good deeds keep the world afloat. My mother was a part-time *lamed-vovnik*. Wasn't she? Aren't we all? My mother was someone who was born and gave birth and died.

When will the last trace of my mother disappear? The mirrors were covered, covered with sheets; it's so hard to find plain white sheets nowadays, I had to run out to Kmart real quick to buy some. My mother hadn't wanted to cover the mirrors when my father died, so we didn't. Superstition, she'd said. After we'd covered all the mirrors in the house I didn't know if I was myself or my mother. For the seven days of shiva we all sat in the living room on boxes and low stools. It felt familiar. It was familiar.

There are closets to go through and drawers and scrapbooks, the refrigerator, too. But now the refrigerator is full of casseroles and bagels and cheeses and tomatoes, coffee cakes with pecans and thick swirls of cinnamon icing. And boiled eggs, a sign of the cyclical nature of life. They are traditionally served after a Jewish funeral, but now no one wants to eat eggs because of the cholesterol. The egg is dangerous. But they took big wedges of pound cake, chocolate Bundt cake, chocolate truffles to die for. They were the same people who came to my father's funeral, Ellen and I will write the same thank-you notes to them, just the two of us writing and addressing them this time. One of us will figure out where to get the cards engraved. The family of ———— thanks you for your concern/love/understanding/presence at this time. Choose one two three. It is fun to see the cousins. She's out of pain, they all say. A strong lady, they say. Hard these past few years, with Ruben and all.

When I took down the sheets, my grandmother said, Ruthie—Ellen—Ceci—don't forget you have to wash those. Give them to me, baby, give them to me.

## Rose in Her Backyard

It is your art form, I say. The blues and reds, hung just so, swaying or not, depending on the wind, sheets scalloped. The picture is pretty. Pretty as a picture.

Grandma Rose does not agree—to her it is workaday. It is not art. It stretches, two lines of it. Her underwear, housedresses, tablecloth. She is hanging sheets, clothespins in her mouth.

In Chicago one year a man pasted silhouettes of clothespins on light poles and street signs—his way of chasing local fame, and it worked. It is not Rose's way or her chase. Her way is washing, hanging, drying, ironing, folding, putting away. She gathers, unfolds from her basket. Her basket, ancient womansymbol. No, says Rose, a basket is a basket. Sometimes the straws of it catch on the clothes. She'll say, Tsk tsk. She is round, not yet haggard, vital. But no one records her rituals.

They are not rituals, says Rose, it is cleaning. At eighty-five she still mops the floors, using Mr. Clean and ammonia, her own solution. Wipe, squeeze, wipe, squeeze. And what is this, Miss Smarty? she asks. Music? She has not heard of John Cage, though she suspects, or would surmise, that people of his ilk are out there. She is not a Philistine, just suspicious of that which does not seem to be hard work. She does for others. They will do for others, later. And for themselves. That is the way of it. That is how it is done.

Or you can hire out. Except this is mother's work. If you hire out, the girl never does it as well. On sunny days, it is pleasure, not art. Pleasure in the sun, her tiny yard behind her townhouse, a neighbor's dog barking at the clothing, running through, almost pulling off a sheet. The dog knows it is pleasure. Pleasure in the inexorable transformation of slapwet gray clothes to dry, brilliant white. Rose thinks: I did that. I made them that way. I, Rose the caretaker. Taking pains. Taking pains makes it all worthwhile.

Rose has watched her husband and children wear the clothes, had a stake in each shirt on their backs—each shirt like a mayfly, discarded after twenty-four hours. She lost her husband more than thirty years ago. Before his time, but his time just the same. There is nothing to do but what you always do, following the pattern of every day: wash, rinse, spin, dry. Duty and habit will save you from forgetting who you are.

Rose brings clothes back to life, but that is all. Art, no; magic, yes. Rose takes what is thrown into the dirty-clothes basket, fabric marred by sweat and stain, and Rose transforms the cloth, Rose makes it new. Each day is the start of your life, she says. Hang up your clothes, darling, she says. Cut off loose threads. Don't be afraid of perfection. Perfection is possible, says Rose, bending to pin up another sheet, you just have to know what it looks like.

*Part Two*

# In the Beginning

**1**

First, three words about God: He is careless.

He would not last a day as a hired messenger. He would be fired, summarily, without pay. Most of us are in his image. The ones who are neat and take care, they are the ones he would like to be like. They are an expression of his yearning.

**2**

In the beginning was the deadline.

This accounts for many of the mistakes we wring our hands over.

No one can do his best work under so much pressure.

God remains proud of his trees.

**3**

Eve is an orphan. She feels like a starchild plopped down on earth. Adam spends his time on the other side of the garden, digging. Eve weeps for her parents, for her lack of them. She has no one to cradle her. Snake is the only creature who interests her. He rattles his tail, makes himself into a necklace on her bare neck, whispers riddles in her ear, teaches her palindromes. Such as: Madam, I'm Adam. She, in turn, leads him to burrows where rodents hide, where they have scampered in fear of Adam's onslaught. She sings to Snake what she calls the tune of sunlight. Still she does not trust him, makes sure she is always wide awake when Snake winds himself around her bare, freckled neck.

**4**

This is what you will hear, says Snake one day, as he's wrapped himself around Eve's shoulder. It will be passed down that God said you could eat whatever you wanted from anywhere you wanted, but not the apple from the tree of knowledge, and they will say that I am the one who got you to eat it and that will be that.

They will say what? says Eve. They will say that that's all God said, Don't eat from the tree of knowledge? What about all the other rules and regs?

Nope, says Snake. I'm sure of it.

Eve is outraged. Because God is full of rules. This is what God says:

> Don't chew with your mouth full,
> don't talk to Snake,
> let Adam begin conversations,
> don't talk back to Adam,
> be polite when addressing me,
> milk the cows every morning,
> put the cows and goats out to pasture,
> bring them in in the evening,
> feed the animals before you eat,
> strain the milk and churn the butter,
> comb the yaks' fur before your own,
> weed the garden—that's your job, don't shrug it off,
> plant the bulbs and prune the rosebushes when I tell you to,
> harvest and thresh the wheat when it's time,
> don't think about the stars,
> don't let the chipmunks suckle at your breast,
> don't say you're bored,
> don't sing,
> check for lice every morning,
> don't run or dance,
> don't roll in your shit,
> don't pick the roses,
> don't go out of the garden,
> don't tell jokes,
> don't forget yourself,

don't talk about me,
don't discuss your dreams with Snake,
don't sleep with Snake.

And because Eve is talking about God with Snake and has not combed the yaks' fur or weeded the garden or pruned the wildly tangled rosebushes for what seems to God to have been an awfully long time, God descends at that very moment, because he's bored. He hasn't thundered for a while, and has been waiting and waiting for her to pluck that apple, and he figures, Why not get the show on the road. This is what God trumpets, to Eve and Snake, because Adam, as usual, is occupied with trenches and ditches: Because you have disobeyed me at some time or other, you must leave the garden. You must wander the earth's curves and edges, and not look behind you.

So then we can leave the garden? asks Eve, and God doesn't like the quick way she asks that, he feels regret already, but he can't go back on his word, can't change the plot. Eve draws herself up on tiptoe, shades her eyes, squints to see what treasures lie in the unknown. I hear the mice on the other side are nice and juicy, she tells Snake quietly. They'll roll straight into your mouth, soft as velvet, butterballs.

You think so? Snake whispers back.

God clears his throat and says, And this shall be your curse. Listen to me. You will be required to earn your bread by the sweat of your brow.

We do already, says Eve.

You do? God asks. Well, then, you will give birth in great pain and have monthly reminders of that pain.

Eve says, I already have PMS.

You do? God asks. Well, then, you, Snake, you will lose your legs and crawl on your belly like a beast of the field.

I already do, says Snake. Where would I put legs? How many legs would it take to transport the entire length of my body? How would such legs be attached?

You will know death, says God.

We already do, says Eve. Every other day, it seems, we're going to a funeral. It's the cold that does it.

And you, Snake, you will lose your gift of speech. And become but another dumb beast—

—of the field, answers Snake. It's OK, old man, we communicate telepathically, anyway, this girlie and me. We're both Libras.

Then God, who sometimes can think under pressure, rouses himself to pronounce quite formally, as he believes is befitting the supreme lord of the world: You will be banished from the garden, and Adam and Eve will work for a living. And, furthermore, they will know death— even more than they do now. And, furthermore, well, guys, he says, running out of steam, realizing the ridiculousness of referring to his audience in the third person, trying now to be the good cop, I have a favor to ask. After it's all over, you don't have to describe all the . . . uh . . . low points before you left Eden. I mean, among friends, it hasn't been that bad, has it? So if anyone asks what it was like, just tell them everything was perfect, OK? Tell them it was bliss, heaven on earth. Don't tell them, God continues, that you got headaches or cramps or—

—ever got stepped on, Snake offers.

—had to get yourself up at three in the morning to walk to the outhouse in the driving snow. For example, says Eve.

Exactly, says God, we're talking the same language. Tell them, he says, warming to his own rhetoric, that it was one beautiful day after the other, no floods ever but soft gentle rains, and rainbows so frequent but not all the time, rare enough to remain special. Eve, tell them how you loved Adam, how you were equals though you came from him, equal in my eyes, though of course he is my son; don't tell them about the compounds you had to build to keep the lions out; tell them you had chocolate in all its forms, and we're not talking carob; tell them each night you slept better than the next, you ate better, tell them linen, napkins, silver. Don't tell them about the rot in the nuts and berries, the stomachache from the raw cashews, the friends who died from poison mushrooms, the sickness and misery that came from not knowing fire, heat, or warmth. Don't mention the feeling that racked you that you must have done something wrong. Because you always knew you'd transgress, you were bound to. Don't tell them any of that. Tell them it was stupendous, unimaginable; otherwise their lives will be so hopeless they'll end them and I'll be alone all over again.

**5**

Eve and Snake, of course, refuse. That's perjury, says Snake.

So God, in a coup de grâce (he invented the phrase, after all), shakes himself one more time and thunders: Here then is your fate. When I snap my fingers, you will fall fast asleep. And when you awaken, this is what you will remember: a beautiful green-and-silver garden, sunny golden days, sweet gentle animals, ripe tropical fruit, everlasting life, nothing but pleasure, a conniving Snake, a hapless Adam, a wily Eve, and a just God.

And he snaps his fingers, and Adam, on the other side of the garden, and Eve and Snake, on this side of the garden, fall asleep, as do all the other creatures, small and large.

**6**

And God saw that it was good. And the garden disappeared and was replaced by tundra. The next day God rested. And on that day his creatures awakened, outside the garden, and argued and strained and fought and preyed on one another and some were hurt and some died. The day passed, just as every day before had, back to the beginning of life. Except that on that day, when Adam and Eve and Snake and all the other creatures wept and cried out in anguish because their lives were filled with suffering and loss, they were certain, absolutely certain, they were doing so for the very first time.

## Making Heroes, Beginning with One Sentence

The sentence: *A Latin American peasant walks into a bar.*
(A young peasant. From El Salvador.)
*A young El Salvadoran peasant walks into a bar.*
(She is strong. She has birthed her babies all alone.) She knows the secrets of revolutionaries and of long life. These secrets are contradictory. The enemy is in the bar. He sees her beauty and wants her. He smells her beauty and wants her. He wants to taste. Devour.

She kills him.

As he's dying, he says, Why? She says, Because you didn't love me for my soul.

*The Guatemalan peasant walks into a bar.* She is a poet, a builder. She has muscles that gleam in the sunshine. Or in certain moonlit settings. She has birthed her children on her own or she is a midwife. Wants to be midwife of the revolution. Of the nonviolent revolution.

*The Latin American peasant is walking down the street.* It is bright and looks like a painting of a small-town street, anywhere. It could be a dusty Turkish village, sun beating down like tom-toms. Americans in bikinis squinting at the sun.

Coffee like dirt in little white cups, always a sediment, always a stain.

A crew of dishwashers scrubbing like Lady Macbeth.

Pluck out the source of discontent: *Revolutsia!*

*The sleek young Nicaraguan woman is reading Kafka.* Is reading Eleanor Roosevelt. Is reading Rubén Darío, is reading Cardenal and translating folktales and Indian stories and songs into Spanish. She is on her way to make a CD to sell for her people. For medical aid, which is still needed more than ever under the new regime. Or, frankly, to pay for guns, when the time is right. Guns *are* butter, she tells American audiences.

And vice versa.

*The peasant hero was born in the provinces.* She taught herself to read. She taught herself everything that is worthwhile. The sun taught her everything she forgot to teach herself.

The sheep and cows follow her with their deep brown eyes. She is part cow part sheep part of everything. She loves her country. But with an inclusive love. She has purged capitalism from her heart.

*Or she was born in the city.*

Her name is Rosa.

She knows European vacations. Boarding schools. Father's private plane. Father, big and hearty, hooknosed, curly dark hair, like a mafioso with a good conscience, expansive, singing in a deep voice, preceded by his deep laugh, rich as gravy, singing Rodgers and Hammerstein at dinner, even with guests who didn't know American music. Rosa brought back T-shirts from prep school, gave them to her friends, to the maid, equality through education. She thought of somehow sending the maid to school, had read Frederick Douglass by then, about the master's wife from the North who schooled him, deliberately unaware she was breaking the law.

They summoned the maid to the table by a bell.

On weekends the father drove the car (the finest Thunderbird in the country, he claimed—admittedly a small, a poor country; he is the quintessential big fish) up and around the mountains. Safe, safe, he laughed, no rebels here. That laugh: Auhu uhuh uhuah. Cringing in the backseat. This is my father. He makes me sick. Hated herself for feeling that way. She always had. Her father like a cloud that always followed her thoughts, shadowed her like the security force. She always looked up in the sky when she heard a motor. He'd done stranger things. He swooped down for her graduation from tenth grade at Hotchkiss. Everyone in a circle on the lawn, him landing on the side (aimed for the middle, she was sure), a Kennedy cousin there, a movie director's daughter, and five diplomats' kids. Huhhuhuhuh. The man with elephant skin. No legal bullet could penetrate it. She tried to make her eyes look daggers. Imagined them like swords in tarot cards.

A woman walks into a bar looking for love.

Young and lovely, the girl from Latin America goes walking, and when she walks, she looks but she doesn't see.

Rosa is young and lovely and could be called Hispanic. Her grandparents were Polish, Ashkenazi Jews on their way to the Statue of Liberty, held back by quotas on East European refugees. Detained in the land of swaying palms. Where more Jews came and waited, until after two generations there was a supple middle class of businessmen, two synagogues (Sephardic and Ashkenazi), and three pockets of town where the Jews lived. Few settled outside the capital.

They educated their children in private schools at home or in secular boarding schools abroad, mingling and hobnobbing with the governing class in many countries, including their own. Citizens of the world, they felt uneasier in their own country than did their Gentile neighbors but blended in more smoothly when they ventured to other continents. With the help of their charming accents, they had refined the art of getting along.

When she was eight, Rosa was sent North to summer camp. She was small and graceful and could do the butterfly kick. Sometimes she'd call it butterfly click by mistake and the kids would laugh. The boys liked her well enough but she was not belle of the camp. She was good at canoeing and for some reason they started calling her Pecan and then Paco. Every once in a while—Spick. Some people thought she was American, they confused her country with Puerto Rico. After camp was over, she sent postcards to her bunkmates for maybe six months. She kept the addresses and sent cream-colored announcements when she graduated from Hotchkiss. She didn't go back to camp. The camp disappeared, in fact. It disbanded or deincorporated, or merely was sold, after that summer. Someone had died, the sister of a camper in the next cabin. She knew the sister better than she had known the dead girl. The sister knew Rosa's name. The dead girl's name was Lori and that was the first time Rosa heard the term *death seat*. Lori was sitting in it on her way back from the dentist's office in Town—a collision. A counselor was driving. Rosa didn't remember if Lori was wearing a seat belt or who in particular was driving or whose fault it was. She was Jewish. So were most if not all of the campers and almost all of the counselors, though some of them were local Missouri girls and boys. Rosa's counselor was a baton twirler, for instance, from the next county. Non-Jew. And they all wore white to the memorial service that Friday night. Uncle Ted, the owner of the camp, read some poems the dead girl had written. Lori's sister Randi or Mandi decided to stay at camp. Her parents called her every night.

Lori's mother: If someone dies of an overdose, for example, or from a car accident in your town or even on the highway it's one thing, you never think she'll get hurt if you send her to a place she loves, out in the country.

You think, She loved it, but if only she could have stayed home this year or if she could have waited to get the braces fixed, but it was hurting, Ma, that's what she said. Our last conversation with her, she talked about going to town because she'd evidently had steak and corn on the cob and popcorn and we said, Fine, do you have the money to pay for it? And she said, Don't worry it's only ten or fifteen dollars. We said, Well, don't hesitate, go when you can—anyone would say that, wouldn't they? If it was your daughter and the wire was scratching into her cheek and she joked about cutting it herself with wire cutters or pliers—.

We said, We should send you to dental camp so you could learn how to do it yourself, and I thought of specialization and my parents who were socialists and how they feel about doctors in general and the AMA's fight against national health insurance. Every time we complained about medical bills they'd rant about the doctors keeping knowledge to themselves, taking away the folk remedies of the people (though who can move teeth like orthodontists?), collusion with government and big business. This was before Watergate, you know. Before most things. It was two summers before the Days of Rage. We'd seen two hippies, both in New York City. The world hadn't turned around on its head. Actually, it never did. We thought it would.

The black hole, the sending of the body, the meeting of the body at the airport.

This is what turned me against the Vietnam War. I thought, If she were a boy, in five years she might be coming back to me like this killed by the Vietcong.

We tried to lay our grief aside but merely coated it over with dailiness. I wanted to squeeze Mandi every time I saw her asleep, brown hair feathering out on the pillow. I knew I might become overprotective, so I went back to radio work, especially so I wouldn't build my life around her. I put all of Lori's pictures away and then one day I put them out again and I thought, I'm not such a bad person even if I can go on with my firstborn, first-bat-mitzvahed, dead.

And the radio station, one that relied on listener donations and time, grew under me like a wildflower. I began sleeping there and hosting three shows and following groups of subscribers and volunteers to the draft board, the state capitol, and the White House, through the streets, shouting until we were hoarse and exhausted and more outraged at the end of each march than we'd been when we'd started.

The mother plowed through her grief and became the person you saw on television, almost an icon, a suburban (read: heretofore not dangerous) woman outraged by the events of the day, arrested time and time again after chaining herself to fences in front of the White House, the Pentagon, the draft-board office, eventually sacrificing her home life, her suburban friends, her privacy, for the Cause. She became a mouthpiece, a woman shouting behind bars.

So that was Rosa's first camp experience in North America. Uncle Ted and Aunt Vicky sent letters to all the parents about the tragedy and said how they'd handled it—one way to keep the rumors from spreading out forever. The next year it was a JCC camp, and a few kids went back, would talk about how this used to be the Crow's Nest and this had been Cedars and this is still the swimming place, can't change that, can they? And they'd think about Lori and about drowning for some reason and never go quite as far into the lake as they had before.

All the clichés are true. Flesh of my flesh, life of my life. You feel disloyal if you do not think of it every instant.

We are trained now. We say, We have one daughter.

*The peasant woman walked into the bar.*

*The grieving peasant woman walked into a bar.*

*A no-longer-grieving woman walked into a bar.* Very tired but determined. Looking for recruits.

Across town the woman, across the town the country, across the country the teenager Rosa again stayed home, her parents hosting their annual party for the American ambassador.

Odd neighborhood, everyone jokes, like always. Because it is. There is their house, brick wall in front of white stucco, which her father built himself twenty-five years ago, along with their grandmother's next door. Hot pink bougainvillea and sunset-colored hibiscus drape the walls and cover the courtyard, a jungle of caresses. Across the street are little hardware stores and *limonade* places, ramshackle, and a few little houses, tilting so much you'd think they wouldn't survive the next big rain.

Your father is good to you, her mother says, reproaching. She always says this because they are always saying Daddy—in the U.S. fashion, as he trained them—did this or I wish Daddy didn't do this. Sometimes they even call him Father. He might think it's respectful. Rosa's little sister Lili doesn't say much now. She's somehow gone inward. She still keeps her dolls and she's already twelve.

Who do we play with out here? No one. In the summers I come home from boarding school and go swimming with my cousins. Then we travel, a happy family from Latin America. Smashing the stereo-type. No we're not poor. They think we're Americans. They don't know we're Jewish.

In Lucerne I try to lose them, bargain a morning by myself, and stretch it into an afternoon, walking along Lake Lucerne feeding swans. I look for saviors. There is a blond man with shaggy hair, tall. Alone. He doesn't speak to me. I think how I would rebuff him. Then I think how we would drink tea in one of those cafés with striped awnings and Cinzano parasols on the tables. Or inside where it's smoky from filterless cigarettes, like the existentialists' cafés in Paris, like the expressionists in Berlin before the war, just before it got dangerous for Jews to speak, the whole mix of everyone, journalists, play-wrights, inventors of atonality—with their sharp warped analysis of art and life and politics. Politics—I can hear the word, can smell it, it is a sharp acrid Camels cigarette and dark muddy espresso. I can taste the whirl of ideas. I look at tulips. There is no smell. Searching in vain for a smell. Trying to draw its smell out of them. I look at the black stamen and for some reason I start to cry. Why are you crying, young beautiful one? Because the stamen is black and it should be yel-low? Come, let me dry your eyes.

But no one approaches me, daughter of the center of America of the middle of Europe, who has always lived where she doesn't belong. Paco at camp somewhere in the Ozarks. I thought *Ozarks* was the name of a state, one I'd somehow missed in geography. I didn't know it was a mountain or hill range until the third week. Always afraid to ask. She doesn't talk in class, yet she is bright and her papers are well reasoned. They all say this.

In the end, he finances my escape. Northwestern, a good university just north of Chicago—he can land at Palwaukee nearby and rent a car and drive me to my all-girl dormitory.

Oh, are you Hispanic? Oh, is that in Mexico? Oh, is that near the Virgin Islands? (Thinking for a flash they are asking me something else.)

We sit on their sorority-house couches and drink punch and eat cookies or popcorn. The sorority girls sit on sorority-house gray car-pet and ask questions, tell us about majors and gut courses and formals on boats downtown and the sponsorship of a Girl Scout troop and a poor poverty-stricken orphan in Nepal. Or maybe, they say, it's Nicaragua, it's hard to remember which. I think they must be joking. They ask again where I'm from, say Your English is so good—were you born there, is your father a diplomat—and sometimes they speak very slowly and loudly and sometimes so fast between smacks of chewing gum and I can't understand. Then they ask me back again and there are more parties and then we start laughing and they like my clothes and jewelry and I choose and they choose and then I belong. I am a pledge. I become a member.

One night we sit in someone's room with the lights out and some-one passes around a candle and we say, For the good and welfare of our sisterhood——. And we pass the candle around and speak. Then we play truth. They ask, Who do you love? Who do you hate? Someone tells about another group that used to demand, individually as part of pledging, Say who do you love, and everyone named parents, boy-friends, country, self, the sorority itself, until finally they realized the right answer was to echo, Who do you love? Say it: Who do you love?

And then I notice they are moving around me quickly, saying things loudly at me. Because I have been quiet, have been all this time thinking, thinking to myself: Who do I love? Who do I hate? I love my father, no I don't, I hate him. And every night he would kiss me good night, saying, I love you, your father loves you his daughter, don't you want to be happy don't you want me to be happy don't you want to kiss your father good night. And I never wanted to but I did. Just good night on the cheek. A little kiss. That was all. But I hated. Hated that. And his laugh that rumbled through the house and the town and the loud car and just the loudness of him. Yes, that is my father, the loud man there. At home, on vacation, the one strangers notice. They roll their eyes, smirk. And now I am in the Middle West of America and I am away from all that, I am loud myself, I am laughing, laughing, because I am here, with this family, this family of girls, girl-women. I don't have to go home. I am free.

We stay up all night laughing and whispering. They explain to me all the jokes I don't get right away. The next day I sleep until the after-noon. I have a slight fever and my hands are puffy and my roommate makes me go to student health. All the doctors are women and they say, Are you homesick? Are you eating properly? And I say I'm fine, but I start to cry and a woman who is Welsh and hard to understand says, Crying is natural when you're away from home, in another country. And I say, No, here I have a home, with these girls, with this sorority, this all-girl dorm, but the thing is I don't want to go home, I hate home.

Are the girls nice to you? Oh yes oh yes, I say, They are my lifeboat, they are my savinggrace, giggling at the word for it is new and I'm wondering if I'm saying it right. And the woman doctor says, You must stay with them if it makes you feel safe. Your country is the one with the upheavals, isn't it, or is it a neighboring nation? And she tells me to come back to see the psychologist, but I don't make the appointment.

Then come midterms and no one is still shy around me, looking at me like I'm a lame lost puppy. I am a coed. I read the books twice to swallow all their meaning.

In November I begin to dream of being shot in the ribs, of sticking my toe in the mouth of the pistol to stop it. I am riddled with bullets and no one helps.


I am going home for winter vacation. The weather is bad and my mother persuades my father not to get me in his plane. First I spend a week in Cleveland with a friend. She drives me slowly to the airport. Call me if you want, she says, there's not that much of a time difference. She squeezes my hand. I feel I am leaving my home country, the U.S.A.

Then we are in my father's familiar car. I feel the plastic seat covers sticking to the back of my legs but that is all I feel. I am back here at home, I tell myself, but I am not here. He begins singing Chicago Chicago is my kind of town Chicago is, and then, What's the matter, don't you like songs about Chicago, Illinois? He imitates the Chicago accent perfectly, like the perfect mimic everyone says he is. Then he sings, It's a lovely day in Managua Nicaragua. Then, They're rioting in Africa, only he changes all the words so it's in our neighborhood. Oh honey, says my mother. But it's true. I have read about it at school. The underground is plotting.

He is a millionaire. It says so on his gold plaque at the office. No no, he says, he's done a million dollars in trade. Import export, all goes through his hands. He doesn't have it. At least not from there, I think. He wears the gold badge with the dollar sign on his lapel. For some reason I think of people who were protected from bullets in wartime by St. Christopher medals.

Tonight we are having a Hanukkah party for the cousins. My uncle brings spray-painted gold walnuts. We spin the dreidl—a great miracle happened here—light the sixth candle on the menorah. Lili is quieter. I want to ask her if she feels at home at home, if she wants to come to America, if she feels she belongs here, but I don't.

It is dark in our bedroom and I imagine myself saying, Do you like living here? Do you mind telling Daddy you love him? I want to ask her if I am an unnatural daughter for not liking my father. Can she read the shame on my face? She is quiet. I think she is asleep. Even if she wasn't asleep, I couldn't make the bridge from thinking to saying. As if I am missing some crucial cells that would make speaking possible.

The next night is the annual party for the American ambassador. Lili and I go out to a movie, looking at the shopwindows on the way there, talking in short, slow sentences about the movie on the way back. Somehow words seep through my heaviness. I feel I am swimming, carrying weights in all my bones, talking in a code. We stand a minute in the front yard. The house looks beautiful, the way Americans expect it to—little pink lanterns swinging from everywhere. From inside comes the sound of the same quartet that's hired every year to play Bach. We find ourselves at the open door bathed in lights. My father greets us with his big laugh and then brings me to the near-familiar wrinkle-faced man with a gray suit and blue tie. Mr. Ambassador, my father says, this is *our* ambassador, little Rosa is studying in Chicago. For a minute I think my father will burst into song—I can't help it, I'm a songbird, he always says—but he doesn't. The ambassador shakes my hand, asks what am I studying, then turns away to spear a marinated artichoke heart. I am wandering through the mix of smoke and languages and perfume and music, aware that for the sake of history, of politics, I should be calculating whether there is more worry, more hush, than last year, but I feel confused—everything is filtered through my new strange thickness. In the kitchen I tell our maid about the sorority, explaining the songs we have to learn and our mascot, how we all sit together around a tablecloth at dinner and how everyone meets in the library at nine. It's a club, she says. But it's more than a club, I'm trying to get her to see. It's like a family, I say. Ah, she says, nodding. A group of friends. And they all speak Spanish? No, I say, we speak English. And there is a president, it's more organized than just a group. It has a name, I say, a Greek name.

And then in the next room there are huge gruff shouts. Then it is quiet. Then two little shrieks. Then someone turns the stereo on loud and I am frozen. Burglars. The rebels. Why couldn't my father have had this party at the club?

A man opens the swinging door to the kitchen and I see blue jeans and a red bandanna and I know it's the rebels. Three men are behind him and they are wearing Adidas shoes and I almost want to laugh. Then I think, Where is Lili? I look at his eyes and I know them: a boy who did yardwork for us in the summer. One day in the garden I was sitting and reading and he sat beside me and without saying anything he cupped my breasts, stroking them. I hated that he, a stranger, an outsider, was the one who was making this soft feeling, like being protected in a nest, and I wanted him to go away, but I could not move. We heard a door opening in the house and he leapt up and after that he would never meet my eyes. I felt it had been something of a dare and felt humiliated when I thought of it. As if I were a princess he had somehow bewitched and robbed. Smart for the rebels to use him, I am thinking. He knows the house, our habits. For some reason, that does not make me feel betrayed or angry. I almost admire their calculation. I am only strangely curious, like a spectator at a play where action erupts unexpectedly in the audience.

Now his eyes are staring straight into mine above his bandanna and he says, Go hide in the bathroom. You didn't see anything.

My aunt is in the bathroom and two sons of a cabinet minister. I didn't know they were there. The music outside the door is loud. It sounds like a Brandenburg Concerto, but it's so loud I can't tell anymore. I wonder if they are shooting the ambassador. And my mother. And Daddy. I can't imagine—.

We debate in whispers about keeping the bathroom light on, don't know which would attract more attention, having it on or else switching it off. What if they were looking right at it? I wonder what would happen if I had to pee.

I have a watch. Eleven-thirty. I shake it to make sure it's working. My father always said, We're safe here, no one will rob us in this neighborhood, the rebels would have no reason to come here. . . . I'm just a salesman, an importer. I can smell the boys' sweat. My aunt won't turn her face toward me. I look at the window. It is too small.

Then the music is playing softly. Then not at all. There is the sound of wailing. The door opens. It is my mother, white faced, trying to speak, to gasp, like a fish thrown out of the tank. We hug tightly.

Lili had run out the back. She is crying and covered with dirt.

After the funeral I return to school. My uncle takes me to the airport. My mother and Lili make plans to leave for Miami.

Through it all, I am thinking: My real life is in Chicago. I wonder if I'll think that when I get there.

Why did they do it? Why do they hate us? my mother keeps asking.

I know it was not because we are Jews.

I am in Chicago when I hear of the insurrection. I am sharing a basement apartment with a girl who advertised at the student center for a Third World roommate. She is American but seems to know something about revolution. On the walls are posters with fists. She is busy at night with meetings. I have quit the sorority; I told the girls I have to economize now. Partly it is true. It was hard to get money out of the country. I didn't tell the sorority sisters I was looking for a new family, that I wanted to disappear and emerge as a surprise to myself.

My mother sent me boxes of jewelry hidden inside clothes and books, nestled between my childhood stuffed animals. I put the jewelry in a safety-deposit box. The first month, I visited it every week. Is it safe? I asked the man. What do you think, there'll be revolution? Or an earthquake? Only thing could hurt this would be a nuclear bomb, and then it wouldn't matter.

I felt he expected me to laugh.

I read very little about the revolution. I am glad we don't have a TV. I have already been to one funeral. I don't want to know who has moved into our house, what has become of the club or the Thunderbird car. I hear something of a woman who tricked a general into a hotel room, where her friends shot him. Because he struggled. I wonder if he was ever at our parties. For the cause, she said. On the radio she sounded happy. Happier than I have ever been. All the revolutionaries sound happy. Each has lost family members in the struggle. Yet each sounds renewed, alive.

My roommate and I see a film about colonial Algeria. In the black-and-white streets the people are shouting, waves and waves of shouting, enough to drown out the laughs of a hundred generals. Enough to drown out a thousand songs by Rodgers and Hammerstein. The people surge like the ocean. Like a giant tide whose time has come. Unstoppable, drawn by a million moons.

Afterward we walk to the lake. Wind tears under our parkas. The spray is nearly ice. We wind our scarves over our mouths and necks. It seems that another country, not another state, must be on the other side of the lake. Another world. The waves shout. They are strong cold dancers, hurling themselves against the rocks. But they don't get hurt. Or apologize for slowly slowly wearing down the stone.

I am ready to join something, engage in some wild dance of abandon, but something in me is whispering, Not now, not now. The soul flutters, returns to the roost.

I choose my classes by their reading lists. I learn about the creation of new countries. I read Trotsky's jail poetry and Fanon's hatred and Rosa Luxemburg's protestations that she was born to be a country girl. I become thin and impassioned about justice in the Third World, concentrating on Africa. My father died in the revolution, I sometimes say. I don't say which one or which side.

I do not light a memorial yahrzeit candle for my father. I feel I am the one who has died. Lili and my mother are part of an expatriate group in Miami. The maid visits them. They have made a home there.

It seems more solid than the one my father built—smaller but with the same thick white walls.

I am on scholarship. I had the choice of working in the library or the kitchen of the campus bar-restaurant. I chose the kitchen. I like the steam and the clanging of cheap silverware against thick plates. I feel safe inside when it's cold. I love the quiet crunch of thick snow.

It is early January, the month of the heaviest snows, and I am washing glasses in the soapy water and looking out the window as if I could see the new school term waiting for me out there. I feel I am in perpetual wait, waiting for strength, for some kind of sign telling me what to do next.

Whenever the swinging door opens I can hear the music and smell the smoke and I know one night someone will ask me as I clear the dishes from the oak counter, What are you doing here?

And I will have an answer.

# After the Procession

(during which the child in the crowd shouted, "But the emperor has no clothes!")

At first they were grateful. Exactly as you have heard. "Out of the mouth of a babe," they said. A collective sigh. "We always knew that emperor was a fool."

My outburst had terrified my parents. My mother used to say, "Those few seconds right after you blurted it out, that was the longest silence of my life." And even after the relief of pure, universal acceptance, they stayed scared. They agreed to everything. Let the emperor's court artist paint my picture. We went for dinner with the emperor, who tried to laugh off the whole affair as a joke, even gave me some of the real golden thread that his ministers had repossessed from the thieves—"A souvenir," he said. He called me "a rosy forthright child" and gave me a sweet-smelling crimson bouquet. But his life had changed because of what I had said. He had lost face and soon crept away into early retirement in a country villa.

I cannot say when they turned against me. Who can mark when hairline changes begin? At school the other children teased me, calling me She Who Tells All. Pretended that I had a special way of divining who had done their homework and who had not. Watched my every move. They would not confide in me; I knew too much. They pulled at my clothes. They said I was naked when I was fully dressed. I knew I was not. Then I began to doubt.

The elders began to point me out as I walked through the streets. They said loudly: "There goes the one who caused dissension to rip our community. The common people no longer listen to their superiors," adding that there had been no trouble at all until the child of a lowly tradesman had ridiculed the emperor and his ministers. They wondered aloud why my parents had no other children.

The neighbors shunned us. My father's carpentry business dwindled to orders from just a few loyal friends. I had dreams. You have had them: You are sitting in a schoolroom, stand up in order to leave, realize you are wearing nothing but your undergarments. Or you are at a grand dinner and are completely unclothed, the napkin too small to cover your nakedness. The evil letters came after that, and messages scrawled on the front of our house: "Why did the crops fail this year?" Rumors grew that I had had something to do with the fire at the granary.

My whole life became denial, apology. The people began to miss the emperor. He had been replaced by his brother, a dour, emaciated man who never smiled, rarely showed himself in public. He brought his own ministers with him. They were as pinched up as he was, corrupt, would send their minions to farms in all the districts, demanding the fattest calves and lambs for the emperor's table. They all had accents. The emperor was remembered as jolly, foolish, harmless. He had never raised taxes. He had been benign. Vain, silly, gullible, foppish, but had never meddled too closely in the lives and pockets of his subjects. Laissez-faire, with a giggle.

A clandestine movement grew, determined to bring him back to power. Intrigue swelled, spreading mistrust from household to household. The townspeople began to reminisce about the public circuses and flamboyant harvest festivals, his magnificent wardrobe—seen and unseen. You could hear the muttering: "What was the reason he went into exile, anyway? He was doing a fine job. Until that witchgirl had to open her mouth."

One night men burst into the house, their faces covered with black cloths. They shoved me out of bed, shouting, "That's the one!" They pulled at my arms. "Don't struggle," they said, "We've got ahold of you. You can't get away." My parents stood in the shadows. Feigning yawns. Smoothing each other's nightrobes. I think I heard my mother say, "That child never looked anything like us."

My mouth was gagged, a band tied around my eyes; I was thrown into a wagon that clanged down the cobblestones, into a bare cottage on the outskirts of town. I was fed by anonymous souls in dark rags who would not speak to me. In time, I came to believe that I did not belong with the rest of the townspeople. I signed a petition urging the emperor to return. I agreed to remain in exile. It was right that I be separated from the community. I felt: Yes, absolutely, I deserved it. I vowed a life of silence, eyes cast down. I swallowed my fate.

# The Frog/Prince

Day after day she sat by the side of the pond and watched for that tongue. If he opens his mouth—now—then she missed it. Watched again like she'd watched for shooting stars by the side of a hill one evening, many summers ago, when her father was only a prince. Back then the whole family could leave the palace without much notice, slip through the back—go on picnics, ride horseback under the clouds, sail small boats on the lake, almost as if they were normal citizens. Cousins everywhere, no one aware of rank. When her father became king she became alone. She wandered the grounds. He gained a kingdom, she lost hers—lost her school in exchange for a tutor, exchanged crowds of cousins for ladies-in-waiting. There was no one who was her peer in the entire kingdom. When it came time for her betrothal, a call would be sent to all the neighboring lands that were at peace with her country.

Mornings she sat by the pond reading a library book about amphibians. She wished she had checked it out from a public library, but it was from the royal library, a dark house of rooms and ladders. She could get whatever she wanted there. When she chose a book, the librarians put a red strip of paper in its place on the shelves. That was her color, red; she thought at first, proudly, They know I am fire, but she found out later that there was no system, the library staff used red paper for everyone, until the red paper ran out and the royal librarians went to the next shelves, where the green and yellow paper was kept.

The tongue, she knew, was sticky and pink and it reminded her of paper streamers, party horns you blew. She watched the tongue, wanted to watch it trap a fly or mosquito or too-venturesome water bug, leaping up minutely from the surface. What she wanted was to be small, unnoticed, like the frog, to perch on a lily pad, stick out her long pink pillow of tongue and meet her unsuspecting dinner, jump below the surface for a swim, for a drink, to have everything she needed right there ready for her if she would just rise or dip to meet it. She could swim already and sometimes she opened her mouth to see what would fly in, but she hated the crunchy light texture of bugs in her mouth; the taste she felt she could get used to. She wanted to be one of many, like that frog; was he even the same frog every day? She noticed something flashy on his head, almost a crown; it shone when the midday sun was strong.

She schemed the way girls are taught to scheme. She took oranges with her to the edge of the pond, practiced juggling. She thought perhaps the smell would interest the frog; they have noses, don't they? Or perhaps bugs would fly to the scent of the orange oil on her fingers, and the frog would follow. She watched him watching flies, not watching her. Even when she dropped oranges in the water, accidents each time of course, he merely blinked at the plash, turned his head.

At home at the palace, she crept up to the centerpiece on a hallway table, a golden bowl. From the bowl she plucked a hollow golden ball, a gift from a faraway noble, hid the ball in her pocket. She scampered back outside, out to the edge of the pool, threw the golden ball up into the air, clapped her hands. A game, to build the number of claps. Then she went home. The third day of playing with the ball she let it fly from her into the water. It was heavy enough to sink just under the surface. She cried loudly, of course. Asked the frog if he would retrieve it. I will spend a day with you, she said, bring you choice spiders from the king's garden, I will swim underneath and around you—aren't you lonely, I never see you with anyone, another frog around you—. She was babbling. He simply dipped himself down and pushed the ball with his nose, toward her, till it landed on the shore. What I want, he said, is to spend a day with you, to be carried upon a pillow, to eat from your silver spoon, sleep by the edge of your bed. I want to be dry, indoors, eat soft orange and red and green foods. She rejoiced. A day in the palace together, she imagined, followed by a day, days, a life in the pond with him, naked swimming, no ladies-in-waiting. He would tell her the secrets of being on land and water, what it was like not to need anyone else, how he sustained himself day after day, quiet, still, waiting for prey; she wanted to lay a gluey clump of eggs with black dots like eyes in them, have him add his flash of life to them, watch their tiny black commas of babies, fish, emerge, name them, hear from them how it was to breathe the water through their gills, watch the tadpoles' color and shape and form. All I want, she thought, is to stay in the pond and watch my children transform.

She agreed to let him spend a day with her, and because she had agreed, she played hard to get, as she'd been taught in her training to be a girl—she ran straight home without looking back. She laid the golden ball carefully among the others in the bowl, washed her hands and face for dinner, let the maids brush her hair. Sat at the table, heart beating as she waited for the door to open. It did. The frog hopped to the center of the table, she feigned horror of course, he told her father the story of the promise, her father ordered her to keep her promise, ordered a footman to bring him a pillow, ordered her to feed the frog the fruit compote from her silver bowl, ordered her to bring him to her bed. Exactly as she had planned.

In her white lace nightgown, content, the princess laid her head on her pillow, the frog not two feet away on his green velvet bed. She dreamed of carrying him back to the pond. He would beg her to stay outside with him, she would comply, he would kiss her, and she would become as small and wet and green as he was, and no one in the kingdom would find her again.

In the morning he said, You must kiss me. She pretended not to hear. He demanded: You must kiss me or I will call your father and he will make you. She opened her lips, put them to his mouth, made a moue, inched her tongue to the crease of his very thin lips. Would he open his mouth, let her get lost in the stickiness of his tongue?

You know the rest. He turned into a man, tall, blond, dry. He wrapped himself in silks, ermine, so pleased to be in good, dry clothes, away from all that damp. He sent for his entourage. He told the princess she must learn the proper way to address servants and dignitaries. His tongue, she found, was less than ordinary: short, pink-brown, pointed. He was a gourmand, complained about food, too hot, too cold, the spices were off, stale. He said, It is good to be released from that enchantment. He said, We will have blond children, we will send far away for the best tutors. He said, Why do you continue to cry? It is so wearisome. Her father said, You must marry him, his property is full of orchards, rolling hills, strategic mountains.

Late one night she crept to the pond. She stood at the edge of it. She stripped off her royal robes. Dove in. Began to swim, in slow strong strokes, toward the place where it opened up into the river and then to kingdoms uncharted, unknown.

# My Mother's War

My mother was an artist. When I was ten she entered her bone-and-glass period. I would eat pastrami sandwiches in the utility room, the thick smell of boiling beef fat in the kitchen permeating each bite. I held pickles to my nose like ether. Rings of white grease lined the double stainless-steel sinks. She would stand, her French twist unraveling as she blew into the hollow end of leg bone to free the marrow. The marrow was long and slimy inside the splintering bones, which were sharp as the shards of brown, clear, and green glass she collected from the street. (You can't believe how much glass there is outside, she said. You better quit going around barefoot.) In the oven they were supposed to melt together into the kind of threads that glassblowers produce. But it never got hot enough. She couldn't understand this. Why then, she asked, do people spend their money on Pyrex if any old glass in the oven doesn't break or melt?

She glued the glass to the bones. She filled their cavities with ground-up glass, the way other mothers filled turkeys with homemade dressing. She always bought chicken Kiev prestuffed. At other people's houses I would see mothers wrist-deep inside chicken as if they were caught, momentarily, in their own private patches of quicksand.

The reviewers came to the opening of her show. It was in a rented loft above a weaving factory. The man from the *Post* called it brilliant. The woman from the *Chronicle* said it was a sham. That her seven-year-old son working with her three-year-old spaniel could do better, except that they both had more sense than to play with broken glass.

A loudmouth TV anchor ridiculed her for three minutes on the five o'clock news, and everyone I met after that said my name sounded familiar.

At her next show she strung baling wire through the bones. Black lights hung from fishnets. Everywhere was the smell of jasmine. The people who attended the opening were longhaired and bearded, wore muted flowing clothes, and passed around hash pipes. The *Post* critic shared his Acapulco Gold.

Someone called the police.

The *Post* carried the story on the arts page. The *Chronicle* put it on page I. It was an open invitation, my mother said into the phone. We didn't station guard dogs at the door. Middle-class morality, she hissed after she slammed the receiver.

After that she always had to have two opening nights to accommodate the crowds.

Her hippies came to my bat mitzvah. My speech was about Jonah and the whale, or, rather, the great fish, though "Jonah and the whale" sounds better. The story about Jonah is read on Yom Kippur. I was supposed to stick to the Torah portion. But that was about punishment for sorceresses or people who coveted. Nothing a child can relate to, my mother said.

I described the blubber inside the whale. Jonah almost drowned in the fat. This was more frightening than darkness. He felt like he was walking through slimy white mud, through melted chocolate, whipped cream cheese, cakes of softened soap. This was not manna. He could not eat any of it. He was looking for a way out. He struck a match and burned the top of the whale's insides. The whale blew him out of his blowhole.

This proves, I told the congregation, that the search will save you.

Her hippies told her I was a deep thinker.

At the reception, I rested on a chair along the folding partition that separated the social hall from the sanctuary. A boy sat on my lap and fed me stale sponge cake. When he pinched my nipples and said, Milk Duds, I stood up.

He scampered away.

By the time I was fifteen, she was famous. She flew to New York every two weeks. I lived on Sara Lee cheesecake and Mrs. Paul's fish sticks. In the afternoons I skipped algebra and sat on the sloping cement along the bayou and watched the gray-brown flow. There was much green glass.

Senior year I worked in a pet store. I changed straw every day and caught fish in my bare hands. The goldfish beat against my cupped palm like a heart pressed flat. I would take a deep gulp as I tossed it into a plastic bag. I exhaled as I tied the twist-em.

Don't overfeed her, I warned the earnest little kids.

She bought me a Nikon for graduation. She said, Do you want to take a year off? Not everybody goes to college.

I took one year, and it grew to three, four, six. We count what we call life credits, the dough-faced lady at the community college said, like she was explaining the rules for hopscotch. You could get an AA degree in three months. What would you say your specialty is? Philosophy?

Two years later I became an artist-in-the-schools. My fingernails turned yellow and my hands always smelled acrid. I concentrated on portraiture. Look what you can do, I told the kids. Preserve what you see. Paint with light. Capture something and make copies forever.

I would fill in the pictures true-to-life with crayon and copy them on a color Xerox machine. They looked realistic, only rougher. That became my trademark. Postmodern realism, they called it.

Her fame deserted her like a bored lover. She shaved her head and glued her hair to the wall in the living room. She separated the white strands from the black, burning the ends. This took an entire month. If you didn't look closely, you'd think that a small patch of zebra skin was attached to the wall over the couch.

She walked on glass-covered bones barefoot, like an Indian brave.

I am trying to strengthen myself, she said.

I moved to the next state. I became active in community life. I worked my ten hours a month at the food co-op. I joined the artists' collective gallery. I changed the *i* to *y* in my last name. On Sundays I tutored migrant workers' kids. I taught them the game rock-scissors-paper. Sometimes there was a waiting list for me in the artists-in-the-schools program. The students often sent thank-you notes.

When my mother died, her hippies came to the funeral in black suits. At home, they passed around joints and 'ludes. They brought homemade wine and Hershey bars. Chocolate, someone named Lydia said, has a chemical that uplifts you. That is the reason women eat it after breakups. It's therapeutic. Body wisdom.

You could have brought Toblerone, someone said, instead of some corporate product.

Aren't we supposed to boycott them? a man, someone's new lover, asked.

That's Nestlē, a skinny girl said.

The European bars are the best, said the man. I like Cherry Screams.

I think of chocolate-covered cherries. Inside the chocolate is a sugar crust, which holds in the sweet runny syrup and real fruit, round and still red. It is a house inside a house, a bunker, Jonah in his whale.

And what will you do? Cleo asked me, her smile a withered purple between tissue-thin wrinkles.

What I always do, I said.

She's been on her own for years, said someone I didn't recognize.

This is what she left: Scrapbooks of clippings. Invitations to openings. Diploma from Pratt. The certificate of the get, the Jewish divorce.

And instructions for a new show. An environmental piece about the Holocaust. Posthumous. Something that would say, Conceived by Celeste Meieroff, when it opened.

It needed a builder, someone to execute it, a general contractor sort of artist. I advertised in *Art News, American Artist, Present Tense,* and small newsletters. It could be set up and shown anywhere. It was that kind of thing.

The best person lived two states north in a college town. I moved there; all places are the same. I became again an artist-in-the-schools. I located a color copying machine at the print shop downtown. I built another darkroom. On weekends I took pictures of traffic accidents and fires for the newspaper.

I helped the artist write the NEA for a grant application form. When she got the money, I stopped returning her calls. I said I wanted to be surprised.

The artist invited me to see the show on the Sunday before the opening. She left the key to the gallery under the welcome mat. The door opened easily.

I was alone in a dark room. I stripped, like the sign said. The walls were cement block. A yellow lightbulb shone from the ceiling in a black cage. I felt it on my back like a sunlamp.

Metal claws clutched at my clothes. I was not given a claim check.

I waited for a voice over a loudspeaker. Instead I heard a xylophone, the melody from *All Things Considered*, cut short.

The light went out. I waited to sense bodies around me.

So what did you expect? I asked myself. This is the artist's conception of the Holocaust. Did you think she would manufacture crematoria? Kapos, shaved heads, lice—those are cliché. You expect those things. Your aunts and uncles, they didn't know what to expect. Didn't know about the camps and the showers.

They weren't really my aunts and uncles.

Someone's aunts and uncles. They could have been my relatives, if my great-grandfather had not left Galicia. There had been a family dispute. Something about an inheritance. He was disowned.

So there will be no cattle cars. No stench. My mother made her hell antiseptic.

What will the critics say?

Banal? Passé? The art critic on the newspaper also covers drama, dance, photography, music (rock and classical), visiting authors, and beauty pageant winners. I imagine her sitting at her desk, shuffling press releases with her long fingers that end in narrow slices of red. She smokes. Ashes sprinkle themselves on the white papers, filter into the crevices of the computer keyboard. One day the machine will refuse to mark on its screen and the repair people will be dispatched. They will find ash damage. The newspaper will be presented with an ethical problem: Was it the critic's fault?

Yes. But the editor points out that the paper's medical insurance will cover the stop-smoking sessions at Mercy Hospital.

Walk five paces.
No wall.

Five more.

Run, hands out; whenever I float on my back at the Y I always keep an arm extended to rasp against the concrete edge, saving my head. No wall. Counting to one thousand, I run to the left.

No wall.

Blessed art thou, O Lord our God, King of the World, who has created the never-ending universe, extending far beyond our ken.

I begin in Hebrew: *Baruch ata Adonai*—but I can remember only the blessings over Sabbath candles, wine, and bread. And the generic Thank you for enabling us to reach this season.


This is not our Sabbath. It is the Christian Sabbath. The day that nothing is open but 7-Elevens. On Mondays, museums and beauty salons are closed. On Thursdays, retail outlets stay open till nine. Every night except Sunday, the downtown shopping mall is open till nine. White letters proclaim this on the glass doors in front of Penney's: These doors are to remain open at all times during business hours.

What happens to the employee who locks up early? A scolding. He is tired of traffic, of bag-laden shoplifters who graze from department to department, slipping in lacy Hanes and earrings that grow in sharp angles. The girls behind the counter promote these in their many-pierced ears. Pink enamel triangles dancing on turquoise. Hoops. Gold balls.

The Nazis yanked out the Jewish teeth for the gold.

The Jews at the foot of Sinai built a calf of gold.

What did Moses do with the calf?

What did the Nazis do with the gold?

Gold, we are told, is precious because it is fragile. Other elements must be added to bolster it. The human being holds trace elements of everything. Zinc. Uranium. Gold. Silver. Copper. Rubber. Paper, ink. Glass. Inside me is the universe. I am inside a microcosm.

My eyes are the color of a 7-Up bottle, fragments shining in the sun. I loved my mother.

Her whispers coming from the loudspeaker: The exhibit is dedicated to my daughter, because she has been inside whales without a lantern. Behind her lids it is as dark as any Nazi midnight.

The Holocaust is a state of mind, the voice says.

It is wrong. I stand in her limitless night. No stars glitter like broken glass. Dear Lise, says the voice. This is what my world was like, except for the ten years when my arrangement of the discards of life and death brought me into the circus. I made something new and I was rewarded. But the audience went home.

She is attaching her loneliness to the six-million-fold horror of burning. My mother did not wear a tattoo, bore no more distinguishing a characteristic than the pain of abandonment. But even if the Holocaust was the human condition writ large, by attaching her wagon to the black star she refused a chance at happiness.

I do not refuse mine. I do not rejoice at the mutilated: singed hair and broken bits of bone. I do not twist and fray what should be left to rest. I photograph what is. I keep the laws of kosher; I do not cook the lamb in its mother's milk. I do not attach like to unlike. I always focus before shooting.

Lise, you do not create, the voice says. You absorb. Now, I am blinding you with my sorrow.

The Holocaust, says the voice, is my story. It is your story. It is Jonah's story inside the whale.

I remember from my bat mitzvah speech: Seek, seek a way out. In the seeking is the answer.

The child's riddle comes back to me: What would you do if you were inside a brick house with scissors and a piece of paper?

Answer: Cut the paper in half. Two halves make a whole. Crawl out through the hole.

That is art.

# Rabbi Seeking

We are looking for a rabbi. A new rabbi. The last one, everyone said, was a nice man. He was a nice man who wore a nice suit. So easy to talk to, people said. Visitors would leave, visibly impressed, remarking, How remarkable.

But what he said was not important. If it were important it would have transformed us.

He was not what we wanted.

We want a rabbi who's a father. Or at least a husband. We do not want a son. We do not want a son of God. We want someone, like Abraham, who bargains with God. We want someone who can go to the mountain and negotiate for our souls, if need be. Though that is not our daily currency. In America, can you have a spokesman, an instrument of God, when all are created equal under heaven, one-man-one-vote, lack of education or English no barrier to the ballot box? But lo, our instruments are rusted and we cannot hear. Time has rusted them and democracy has rusted them.

We want someone to kindle. Someone to collect the wood, too. Someone who will make us believe in the fire, in the passion of souls, of belief. We want someone who can speak the language, like our grandfathers new in America who would hire someone to write letters for them. We want someone who can extract all the meaning and import from the words, can kindle more from the man-written, God-written texts, who can say, not that he has seen God, but that he has felt God, that he understands what the ancients meant when they talked about a God. Who says that he knows that when we put the word upon God, he evaporates, an animal who disappears from our traps.

The other rabbi was a nice man who wore his nice suit to luncheons, councils, meetings of power, who paid attention to the trappings that make the office pleasant. We want one who is not sullied by closeness to power, who does not have to mention the men of the city or Washington that he has conferred with, the boards he has officiated on, the men he calls by their first names, the women who call him on business. That should not be the business of our rabbi.

We do not want a comedian. We live in a time when comedians joke about rabbis, when comedians blur into rabbis. We embrace as rabbi a Jewish man with a sad face and a philosophy that's deep for America who states his views through his films. But he is not the rabbi. Neither is a witness from out of town our rabbi. We are waiting for the rabbi and we want to make him a messiah. We are waiting for the Messiah and we are getting his son the rabbi.

But we don't believe. We know we're smart (smarter than the rabbi—we know the money isn't in the rabbinate), smart enough to demand a smart rabbi to challenge us and translate for us. To tell us why our ancestors' struggle to hold on to this was important. We want him to tell us they weren't foolish, that there is something precious in the tattered bundles they have left us. We want him to tell us we are not merely blinded by sentiment. We don't want to love this swatch of threads just because it's always been in the family, just because we've had it so long. Tell us it's not fool's gold. We want the rabbi to impress upon us their significance, the way you press a coin into a worthy man's hand. We want the rabbi to walk behind us and say, Look, you dropped this, surely you didn't mean to? Like a redcap of our spiritual lives, we want him to call, Coming through, watch ahead, coming through. Like a prospector, like an appraiser, his light catching the glint of something important among the dust: Yes, there is this tribe called the Jews. And there is something about them. Here is what it is, he will tell us.

THE NEW RABBI:

I am diving for meaning. I am wetting my face, salt clinging and stinging. I delve into waters while they bury themselves in stocks and inventories and blueprints. I plumb the invisible, the symbolic. I am trying to make us whole. It is for my sermons, and for them. The Talmud tells of a fish our ancestors used to dye the fringes of the tallisim blue. Scholars have argued about this creature. Did it have scales or a shell? Did it live in the Dead Sea before it became too salty? Is it Aristotle's *Murex*, Pliny's purple mollusk, a corn-worm, or a louse? Did it de-evolve? Is it perhaps another semantic etymological conundrum, a mistranslation?

What did we do to lose the exact name of this indigo-producing animal? What did we do to lose the recipe?

After I find it, will it mean anything, this snail-darter of the soul? Why all this work, for the sake of the color in a prayer shawl?

Is a grown man allowed to roam this brine? Does a grown man dare admit to his neighbor home from the train that he spent his day searching through books for snails and conches that live on many levels, snails he could not eat for dinner? Alchemy. The lost dye will help us find ourselves. It will tell us what we lost, what we must find to heal. The secretions of the nonkosher mollusk will be balm for our souls.

I do not want to appear eccentric. I do not mention this sea creature to the new congregation. I will present it to them like the first fruits of the harvest.

THE NEW RABBI'S WIFE:

The rabbi's wife does not have room for a profession even if her husband goes to the office every day like anyone else. Even if he is like a professor in that way. The rabbi's wife is his secretary, emissary, scribe, an expert on all household laws, a nanny putting the children through their paces like miniature diplomats. And what does your husband do? the neighbors ask. It has never been second nature in filling out forms even at the dentist's: Spouse's profession. Or at the doctor's, highest priest of all.

I wish he were a king. Or duke. Something more defined. Something that wouldn't get lost in the shopping mall. Does it say *rabbi* on our American Express card? Of course not. At least he's not like one of the crazies who blesses ships and goats and new buildings. He has some dignity of office and he has standards, though they are painful to the congregation: he won't marry anyone who has chosen outside the faith.

THE NEW RABBI:

People on pedestals long to look someone in the eye. My best friends are other rabbis and ministers. It is true, as they say: In a pinch we trade sermons—changing a few key paragraphs. I keep the punch lines.

THE NEW RABBI'S WIFE:

After several years I can joke about his jokes. I can see that he is a man, even if they won't let him be ordinary. But there is no one to tell this to. Every utterance seems a violation. To talk of your husband, the brother of God, in a group of women drinking coffee? I've heard of a group for rabbi's wives. But they are old. They believe too much, in too much. Too deeply. I'm afraid I love too deeply and have already given too much. Part of my childhood rides up with him on the pulpit, wisps of my morning dream in a paragraph of a sermon. Sacred wrapped around profane. I have seen the rabbi in his underwear. Without his underwear, without his glasses. Looking for his glasses. Looking for his underwear. Taking off mine. I have felt his flesh enter into mine, not gently. Joining but not becoming a part of. Announcing itself. I have heard the rabbi's cry of ecstasy when he has taken off his robes, my robes. I wonder, Is this a holy man? Is this a holy act?

I wrestle with him. I am Jacob and he is my angel. My angel, I say. My angel, he says. God is watching. He was there at Cozumel in the honeymoon suite. Though it was no different from night after night at home. Do I love God? No. Do I love this man who loves God? Not enough. Do I believe in the love of God for this man? In the man's love for God? Whom does he love better? Would he die for me? Will he live for me? Who is this God?

THE CONGREGATION:

Do we believe in his belief in this God? Yes. He tells us of his struggle. The wrestling with his angel. We struggle to respect a man who believes in spirits. In other respects, he is so much like other men. The precious rabbis of our imaginings, we carry them in our inner hearts—we remember their thin gray beards, fragile like baby's breath, their bodies thinning to sticks in the camps. The rabbis were made stronger and frailer by their belief. A strong stone of God inside them. Stones of belief. Men of God. We don't know if this is indeed a vocation like any other.

THE NEW RABBI'S WIFE:

Wife of the man of God.

God's daughter-in-law.

This is the modern era. The rabbi drives his car and eats dinner warmed in a microwave. Everyone calls him by his first name. His English name. How goodly are your tents O Jacob, my angel.

He leads the congregation on retreat. On the Sabbath we wade into the lake and jump toward the moon. I follow this man in his jumping toward the light. The water sighs. It is cooler than the hot night air. My children splash and link arms with other children. I hold the waists of the women. I notice how slim their waists are. I wasn't raised to bathe with others, public or private.

THE CONGREGATION:

He showed us the moon. He said we were like the moon, like light, like new fruits, as whole unto ourselves as a great ball of cool light. Through struggle to maintain ourselves, he said, quoting Spinoza, we find ourselves. "The endeavour wherewith everything endeavours to persist in its own being, is nothing else but the actual essence of the thing in question." The running creates the runner, while the thought of running does not. The seeking creates the seeker. The pliant tree in its grasping for air and light and water becomes more of a tree. And stronger.

THE NEW RABBI:

The congregation wears white, discusses during the discussions, takes the aliyahs, they have faith I will lead them where I will lead them. They come wanting with large empty buckets, clattering to my well. I say, Bring your faith and share it. They bring their doubts and their emptiness like a vacuum. And their unhappinesses all alike, all different and wanting. Judaism is not a summer vacation. This life of faith is not easy.

They toil in their banking houses, in cubicles, ordering inventories, measuring. Counting makes the accountant. I am becoming a fisherman, a seeker of substance, of air. I dream of catching this wet animal of word and symbol, chasing inference, seductive leads, tendrils of hints, stealthily rounding corners. I work until late Thursday searching among Maimonides' fishes and not-fishes. For hidden meanings, God's sleight of hand. Buried treasures.

On Friday they work late. On Saturday they sleep or make love all morning.

My wife, married to the house, the life, to the path behind me or beside me—I don't know which anymore—she wants my search to be important, resents my doubts, and I resent hers and try to hide mine, and she feels ashamed for hers, so steps too quietly behind me as I study and search.

THE NEW RABBI'S WIFE:
They see him as a god but he's a man, with clay feet. We are all clay, dust. And the dust I'll brush with the bottom of my foot to make a footprint. Join together, dust of my dust, his rib, our children, our congregation. All leaping.

THE NEW RABBI:
They telephone all evening. As if the man of God is allowed to lay down his head only one night a week. The congregation's doubts lie upon my doorstep. The doubts like dirty laundry, in bundles. The doubts combine with mine and I can't open the door.

THE CONGREGATION:
We are waiting. Always.

THE NEW RABBI'S WIFE:
The doubts combine with his and we can't open the door. He says, Stay inside with me where it's warm. I'm only a man.

I think: The devil was only a man and girls should watch out for cloven hooves. I saw them everywhere. Years ago this man said, Trust me, I will save you—if you agree to save me.

I am only a woman, I said.
I can't tell if he's only a man.

THE NEW RABBI:

I am searching the meaning of this shellfish, the impossible creature of the Messiah, the secret recipe for the perfect color for the perfect fringes of the tallis, the perfect shape of the world. The answer
lies in wait for me somewhere in these books of holy commentaries,
these theories on ancient history, facsimiles of ancient scrolls.

It will lead me to Eden through Ararat and Babel, through gates
and straits and over walls of doubt and faith. It will lead me away but
the purpose is to lead back.

I dream of netting this *Janthina* or *Murex* or *Sepia*, bringing it up to
the bimah, displaying it. What a clever boy, they will say. What a
clever boy.

THE CONGREGATION:
Then we will love him.

THE NEW RABBI:
Then they will love me.

THE NEW RABBI'S WIFE:
Then he will be theirs.

# That Old-Time Religion

### 1. Your Grandparents

It was something your grandparents offered your parents but your parents didn't want. Or wanted deep down but were frightened of. Or they plain hated it. It was dark. Dark, as in Dark Ages: Old women muttering. Old men shaking. Wailing even. A term for that in Yiddish, forgotten, for that bobbing up and down while mumbling Hebrew, turning the pages of the prayer book in accordance with some ancient rhythm. It looked like senility, this standing bent over with closed eyes, lips opening and closing like fish lips. Like lapses into senility. Into the other side. Into the Old Country. Where it was always autumn. Where they gathered wood and were afraid. Where they whispered to one another: It will get worse. They knew it. Three more months of cold. Followed by the cruel spring: pogrom. Flowers, too, made them afraid, for what they portended. There are few words for flowers in Yiddish, few words to differentiate the various species. That's what your mother said, as if in explanation. It is not a springtime language.

Your parents didn't want that. As children in the new country they learned to look up words in a thesaurus. They learned to skip rope. They learned to ask their parents for American money, to hide their heads, to blush at the accents, the syllables too heavy, too much emphasis for this new world. Homemade was too homespun, embarrassing: Ma, don't make me give that to the teacher. Nothing parental was valued, not even praise. The children looked for deception in the old ways and found it: the kosher butcher who mixed the ritually slaughtered with the *traif*, the rabbi who overcharged his tenant, the scholar who never helped out the family business. See, see, it is all superstition and magic.

So they joined a shiny rational synagogue big and clean like a museum. They sent you to classes. And like the other kids you talked during Sunday school, drew pictures, ran away during the break to buy candy. It didn't matter, it wasn't real school.

Your neighborhood was Jewish, that was enough.

### 2. Your Great-Grandparents Who Stayed Wrapped in It

Your great-grandparents, says your mother, clung, and with age they grew fiercer in their beliefs and more remote. They were giants, wrong-headed dragons, who muttered and shuffled on the Sabbath (on the Sabbath they would not allow themselves light; on the Sabbath a Jew cannot make a fire, which means a Jew cannot flip a switch or turn a knob), only in the later years deigning to answer the phone.

### 3. You, Imagine

You learned the holidays, the words, the language, the major holidays at least. But the religion seemed too much like the boys from the neighborhood—they were loud and unaware of their loudness or their history.

In college you go to Quaker meetings, learn pacifism, learn quiet, listening to the inner voice, which is not speaking Hebrew or accented English, but a quiet whisper that has no accent. It is comforting. But colorless.

You love the Catholic Workers who live in houses of hospitality, so pure, so anarchist and giving—but so Catholic.

### 4. Now, of All People, Your Friends

B has a Torah on her coffee table, a Torah originally from Romania, from a synagogue that was closed down. Everyone in her Havurah, her group, takes a turn bringing the Torah home, she says. The Havurah meets in arkless nonsynagogues—people's houses, condo party rooms, Unitarian churches—its members ever changing, nomadic as the tribes in the desert. There are twelve tribes, most are lost. N says, My family were Levites, we could not own land. We were given the cities. You see the golden cities in her eyes. These Havurah members—called Havurim—mix and match the holidays in ways you did not know were allowed: a seder for Tu B'Shevat, the birthday of the trees, during which they eat almonds and fruits in a precise order, according to the thickness of their husks and skins. On Passover they drip red wine from their index fingers and recall ancient women who danced in the desert, beating their tambourines. After Sabbath meals they sing traditional utopian songs: And everyone will sit underneath his vine and fig tree and we will study war no more. At unexplained intervals during the year they are compelled to sing songs by the East European partisans, with gentle Yiddish sounds that speak of grenades, transports, attacks on the Nazis. They form groups to sing to other friends when they buy apartments. Their voices lilt from the corners of each room. They light scented candles, cast to the four directions, burn sage, say Hebrew prayers, *b'rachas* they call them. Buy mezuzahs to nail next to the door. They offer you honey-sweetened challah, droplets reflecting the light. This exotic culture is and is not your own. It is theirs. They offer it to you like a pomegranate, which you are afraid you do not appreciate. You find only seeds, bite too hard, go past the meat of it.

### 5. He

He says, It is right to make love on the Sabbath. His finger on your lips, in your lips, tickling where it is softest, moving slowly slowly like golden honey. If you opened your eyes you would see his fingertips shine.

This is his Sabbath prayer, repeated weekly, religiously, to whoever will listen, to whoever is there, who stays.

### 6. She

She reads to you from the Song of Songs. Slowly, in candlelight. From far away, the scent of almonds, cinnamon. You are drowsy. How wonderful are the little sheep, and stands of wheat, and jewels of this religion, nothing to do but play in it, dance in its lightness and mystery. No one ever told you it was this easy, to fall into it, to become the dancer inside this religion of music. You will lose yourself here, in this poetry, deep and soft as a thick, dark Persian rug.

It is not what you think, she says abruptly. It is not something to get lost in. You must pull at it like taffy. She tries to convince you it is messy. There are contradictions. Evolutions. Histories. Leaders and followers, schools of thought. Wrestling matches with God. Pilpul, the historic debates over the texts. You say, No no, it is chocolate, sweet chocolate, milk chocolate, and close your eyes.

She leaves you.

### 7. You

You are left with the Hebrew. It looks medieval for some reason. It has secrets. You remember the letter *shin*, like a spider missing some legs, and the abbreviation for *Adonai*, God. This new-old language is tiring. How long does it take for familiarity to grow? Everyone else in the Havurah knows the tunes, the variations of tunes, they return from conventions where they learn more tunes. The tunes radiate throughout the United States and Canada. You can't add these tunes to your store from childhood. You stopped saying prayers before bed. God was a cross between Father Time and Santa. You sat on his lap in a store once, though you couldn't have a tree. There were some limits. You could have a bat mitzvah now, R says. It is too late, you say. Everything is too late. It is hopeless and unfair and you don't believe this godstuff for a moment. Save us, we pray, our vineyards, our granaries, bless us with rain? Love our sacrifices? Our slain she-goats? There is no bridge that links then and now.

### 8. The Ones Who Pray

L tells you that he recites the Amidah every morning; some days the short version, very fast. Saying the Amidah, he says, reminds me that there are more things than getting ahead. You are familiar with the Amidah now because it's said at the end of services; you did not know that people read it to themselves in the morning. D says that sometimes the Modeh Ani, the prayer in which you welcome the return of your soul upon waking, comes back to her, like that. M tells you he is going to celebrate Purim with the Chabads, Hasidic Jews, because they know how to have a good time. They drink. Which is required on the festival of Purim. K invites you to a bar mitzvah. At the synagogue you meet a religious couple who invite you for lunch. They feed you salmon from a tin, the gray-black fat sitting atop it. They crunch the vertebrae. Urge the sweet Mogen David on you. The only true Jews, they say, are the ones who know the precepts and follow them. You cannot pick and choose what's convenient. God wrote the Bible, they say, before the events in it happened. They are not kidding. God is their schoolmaster. They see him with gray beard and staff. They know all the rules. They feel the ubiquity of heavenly cause and effect. All evil, they say, even daily lapses of faith, is punished. God knows everything.

You will not accept the Bible as preordained screenplay. Your parents were right to chuck this handed-down superstition. They were right to turn their backs on this blind following of ancient regulations.

### 9. Your Parents

They thought they gave you a good Jewish life, a good Jewish education. They gave you a Jewish society, where meaning was hidden, like the treasure in folktales. In a Hasidic folktale, a man travels the world and returns home to find the treasure chest buried in his hearth. This idea is universal, the story found in many cultures.

### 10. Your Lips

Move your lips. It doesn't matter whether the tune was authorized at a convention. It doesn't matter whether the words were imported from the Old Country. Move your lips. Hear the echoes. Say something. Anything. Sing. Everything. Sing.

## About the Author

S.L. Wisenberg is a graduate of the University of Iowa Writers' Workshop. Her award-winning stories have appeared in the *New Yorker*, the *North American Review*, *Tikkun*, and numerous anthologies, including *The 1997 Pushcart Prize XXI*. She is a freelance writer and leads writing workshops in Chicago.